The Perfection of Things

Peter Nash

Fomite
Burlington, VT

Cover photograph: House of Stefan and Lotte Zweig, Petrópolis, Brazil, 1942.

ISBN-13: 978-1-944388-33-1
Library of Congress Control Number: 2018937038

Fomite
58 Peru Street
Burlington, VT 05401
www.fomitepress.com

For Annie, Ezra, and Isaiah

Do you know the land where the lemon trees bloom,
And the golden oranges glitter in the dark?

Johann Wolfgang von Goethe

Nothing escapes the perfection of things…

Clarice Lispector

...a brilliant conjuring trick to produce something

apparently orderly out of chaos, to establish a vantage

point from which chance might begin to look like necessity...

László Krasznahorkai

❖ February 21

It is almost dark, Yaniv; soon I'll gather my things and go.

Here in Petrópolis the night is hot, humid, the sky smudged with clouds. Nothing stirs the air, so that even the chimes in the kitchen window are still. This too seems auspicious to me, as if the earth too is holding its breath, so that I am tempted to have another look at the house across the way, to part the pale gray curtains here and mark its place on the hill, but resist the urge, chewing my nails, chewing the weeds of superstition that bind me like a drug.

For how else to explain my good fortune, my luck? It's as if Time itself had stumbled to my aid, had, with its finely feathered hands, kept the contractors and workmen at bay, then coaxed one of them, a short, dark-skinned man with a cross on his neck, to remark to me, to mention in passing, in disgust, snorting a plume of yellow smoke as he hitched up his pants, something about a missing permit or title, about a man in an office somewhere, some lien, some license, some deed, news I was happy, relieved to hear, indeed grateful for, standing there in the lightly spackled sunshine with him, shuffling my feet, while discreetly appraising his hands, the cross on his neck, his perilous ash, the cigarette pinched with a grimace between his fleshy lips, was in fact surprised, perplexed, by his sudden candor with me, a stranger, a perfect stranger in the street, to whom he owed nothing, not *Oi*, not *Bom dia*, not even the time of day, so that he might have just ignored me, turned away, gone about his work, but he hadn't, he'd smiled, he'd grinned at me instead, perhaps feeling good about the morning, there in the sunlight with his cigarettes and coffee, perhaps having slept well, having made love to his girlfriend or wife, perhaps simply stirred by the flocks of pretty schoolgirls who'd passed us in the street, who knows, who can say what reasons, what triggers, only that he'd chosen to address me that day, had pointed to the empty house on the hill and addressed me where I'd stood, where I'd stopped with my newspaper and coffee to consider the temporary fencing, had told me without pretense or prompting, picking a bit of tobacco from the tip of his tongue, what little he knew about the plans, the construction, about this brief, if fortuitous delay, information I would never have solicited, details, intelligence, for which I had never even hoped, having, in my daily encounters with my neighbors, and with the various people in the street, deliberately avoided the workmen and contractors who'd begun to appear at the house each morning, sometimes two or three, with blueprints and cameras, with transits and levels and chains, sometimes as many as seven or eight, with wheelbarrows and shovels and picks, pleased in the main to watch them from my window here, aloof, obscure, adrift at my desk, not wishing to press my luck with them, to arouse their suspicion, to intrigue the builder, the developer, the police, who now, in the name of decency (last week someone painted a swastika on the dumpster out front), who now, in the name of the law, stand bristle-backed before the microphones and cameras, their tails in the air.

In fact they've recently tightened the security around the property, reinforcing the makeshift gates and posting a lone surveillance camera at the top of the driveway (the angle of which I've adjusted to suit me), though the effort seems largely for show. Surely not a one of them has ever read Zweig or will (Dead here? Dead how?), but no matter: the law. The law! Three times now they have blocked off the steps and repaired the chain-link fencing, weaving razor wire along the top. I have watched the inspectors prowling the grounds of the empty house, jiggling the door locks and windows, even climbing onto the roof to assess the mystery from there. No doubt they think it is kids.

Yesterday I was surprised to see a police car stopped out front, though the female officer never even opened her door, only talked for a moment on her cell phone before making a U-turn in the street.

Of course she'd suspected nothing, had never seen me before, never considered my presence here at all—who I am, where I'm from, what I'm doing in Brazil, in this apartment on Rua Gonçalves Dias, where I've been living for close to five weeks now, reading, writing, and staring out the window at the house across the street. She'd had no idea that once, once upon a time, someone famous had lived there: a writer, a man and his wife, a humanist, a pacifist, a suicide, a Jew, having seen only the fence and no trespassing signs, the squat dilapidated house, the hydrangeas in bloom on the hill, knowing little or nothing about Freud or Hitler, about Erasmus of Rotterdam, about longing and sadness, *Schwermut*, a child in uniform really, a child with a badge and gun, having noticed only what she'd been trained to look for, to see, and, not seeing it, shut her eyes, gone blind. It is likely she hadn't even noticed the construction sign at the base of the steep driveway or had noticed it, the dark green color, the tasteful Avenir font, but had not bothered to read it, to consider its implications (the future, the change).

And no wonder, for the renovation has not yet begun, the property—neglected and largely overgrown—much as it has been since World War II. In fact the only obvious alteration, since the last time I was here, is the construction sign itself, which she may or may not have seen, the handsome green sign erected at the base of the steep driveway by one Mario Azevedo, Arq. & Construção, the firm commissioned to do the work.

Not for the first time, I wonder if my entire approach to describing Zweig hasn't been misguided, wrong. I picture the bats in the trees above his house, their jointed, elastic wings, their fitful turns and dives, an anatomy and choreography refined—perfected—over some fifty million years, and cannot help but think of Zweig himself, of the fateful evolution of flesh.

As usual I can hear the television next door: Lurdes, my landlady, is watching her favorite *telenovela*, a popular melodrama based on the novel, *A Escrava Isaura*, by the celebrated Brazilian writer, Bernardo Guimarães. Isaura, the beautiful light-skinned daughter of a Portuguese worker and a freed black slave, is herself enslaved by a ruthless plantation owner who seeks to make her his concubine, teasing her and threatening her until finally she is rescued by her handsome, star-crossed lover, Álvaro. Each evening through the wall I hear the shouting and weeping, picture the slaves and slave hunters, the prostitutes, soldiers, and priests. There is even a hunchbacked dwarf.

Lurdes came to sit with me today to talk about the show, about its latest twists and turns, though she knows the story by heart. And she came to talk to me about her son, Francisco José, who lives with a widow and her children in a slum near São Paulo, babbling away at me with her rings and gold teeth in a curious hodgepodge of Portuguese, English, French, and Macanese, the creole language bequeathed to her in fragments by her Chinese mother from Macau. Her worries are every mother's worries.

Despite my protests, she brought me more food today, some rice and cookies and a dish she calls *vatapá*, a creamy stew of fish, coconut milk, and peanuts I have come to love, though now the smell of it sickens me. Simple smells make me gag: toothpaste, floor wax, gasoline, even the raw, ripe fruit piled high before the little markets on every corner, so that, while I used to wander the city each day, peering into shops and gardens, climbing hill after hill, a ghost to myself, a wraith to the dogs and children at play by the canals with their thick, still water and dark-flowering trees, only to settle for a lunch of fried cod or cassava in some backstreet café, I find myself venturing out from the apartment less and less these days. A strange weariness has crept over me, so that some mornings I haven't even the strength to sleep, let alone to dream, but lie naked all day beneath the window, smoking cigarettes and talking aloud to the world, long, fractured philippics that require no effort on my part, no thinking, not even the flexing of lips and tongue, but pour from my mouth, like some thick and filmy dross, leaving me—so I've often felt it—with the curious sensation of flight.

Since this morning I have not been hungry, content with my coffee, some dried fruit, a few spongy milk crackers, and my usual concoction of lime juice and rum. It is too hot to eat, too hot to sleep. A motorcycle roars past beneath the window; I check the clock above the sink: 5:25: still an hour to go.

Restless, more anxious than usual, I light another cigarette, the last in the pack, and take up the book I chanced upon in a used bookshop last week, an abridged edition of Spengler's *The Decline of the West*, a work I've never read and have only heard contemned, so that now it has for me all the attraction of a pornographic tale. Some previous owner named Cohen or Cohn has marked up the pages, underlining words, expressing delight or dismay in a host of cryptic symbols, even blacking out whole phrases, which words I try in vain to decipher by holding the pages to the light. "Is there a logic to history?" Spengler presses me, near the start of his introduction. Hot, impatient, I read a few more pages, though his answer it seems is clear.

The apartment—two small rooms with a kitchen and bath-room—is owned by Lurdes' half-brother, Fernão, a poet and actor who lives most of the year with his lover in Paris, above a Ghanaian barbershop on rue Lepic. From what Lurdes tells me he is obscenely fat, though there is nothing in the apartment to betray the fact. If anything I would have guessed he was thin.

For more than a week now the place has been infested with tiny brown moths that beat themselves against the lampshade on my desk. Even with the windows closed, which at night I cannot bear for long, they seem to find their way in, fluttering across my books and papers to the rim of my coffee cup or glass, the depths of which they probe with their needle-like tongues. At first a nuisance, they hardly bother me now, but for the way they keep me from my work. Lurdes tells me it is always this way, at this time of year. She says the moths' wings are their ears, that they flutter them to hear.

My neighbor upstairs is playing his Scriabin again, always at this time of night, one of Scriabin's Études, perhaps my favorite of all, No. 5 in C sharp minor, a piece he often plays, though the tenants complain, though the tenants detest it, banging on his door and pounding the walls and ceilings with their brooms. Yet old Vygotsky doesn't seem to mind, to even hear them, their banging and shouting, their churlish cursing at his door, so that I've often pictured the tiny white-haired man poised like an elf before the dingy keys, eyes closed, ears deaf, bobbing gently in the air.

The apartments, built without interest on a slender wedge of earth, are filled with such tenants, men and women whose roots are clearly elsewhere. On the first floor resides an old Indian couple, Bengalis, I think, who live simply, demurely; they keep pigeons on the roof. Around noon I can always find Mr. Chatterjee by the dented mailboxes downstairs, where he likes to wait for their letters from home, happily diverted, astride his collapsible stool, by the crackling news on his pocket-sized radio and by the classifieds in the local paper. Just beneath my apartment lives a red-faced South African by the name of Loots, a young man, a scientist of some sort, who is often away, collecting data about infectious waste. Then there is the Greek family that occupies two large apartments on the second floor. *Senhora* Christakos, whom I often meet in passing on the stairs, muttering and chuckling to herself, seems to do nothing but launder their clothes, which she lugs to the rooftop to dry in the light. She'd never heard of Zweig, she'd confessed to me one morning, dabbing at the sweat on her neck. I know that one of her daughters is deaf.

Rising to the window now I consider the house across the street. This time I'll try the back way in; no one will see me there. I'll skirt the wall between the property and the low, shuttered restaurant next door, then scramble my way up the steep embankment where they've cut back the hydrangeas in preparation for digging. Once on top I should be able to squeeze my way in through the jury-rigged gate.

At first I'd been surprised to learn that they'd detected an intruder, for each time I enter the house I am careful not to leave a trace, patient, fastidious about covering my tracks. I never force a door or window, but tickle the locks until they spring with a click. For I am neither vandal nor thief—unless the past itself is something one can steal. Of that I stuff my pockets full; each night I cram it like soft, sweet pastry down my throat. And I can hear it, too, the past, can smell it, feel its tiny tendrils on my skin. Each night I have only to close my eyes and wait; each night I have only to be patient for the whispering to begin.

Even in the darkness I know the feel of every knob and faucet, every crack and molding, every lintel, mullion, and sill. In my many nights inside the house I've become an expert on termites and woodworm, a pundit of plaster and dust. Every sound enchants: the creaks and clicking, the scratching of palm fronds, the gossip of mice in the walls. The city itself sounds different from there, from deep inside the rooms; once there, once inside, I listen with wonder to the people in the street, to the angry sputter of trucks and motorbikes as they climb the long hill past the house, and if I try—closing my eyes and straining my ears—I can make out the distant keening of gulls.

Come darkness the earth signals itself with smells. Each night the air is quickened round me, stirred to pungency by the swiftly failing light. I smell mildew, old roses, loam lively with spores; and I smell the honey-sick scent of hydrangeas from the tangle above the house, a rampant, bushy-blue variety called *Hortensia*, for which Lurdes blames the Germans who once settled these hills.

The Serra dos Órgãos, so named by the Portuguese, it is said, because the hills reminded them of the organ pipes of their cathedrals back home, have attracted over time the likeliest and unlikeliest of sorts, most of whom have settled here, in this valley, this city, distraught and exhausted, in flight from something or someone somewhere. I often meet them while out walking, and in the bar across the street, where they sit without sense or sorrow, staring at their laptops and cell phones, eyes as empty as shells on a beach.

It's funny what one sees here, the sprites and apparitions. Lurdes glimpsed her fox again last night, trotting its way up the street. A fox, here in Petrópolis! Yet who I am to doubt her, to care? Once near dusk I spotted Bishop and Lota eating figs beneath a tree.

Then there is Dom Pedro II, the last Brazilian emperor; dutiful, heirless Dom Pedro with his small sad eyes and great white beard; surly, bookish Dom Pedro with his Sanskrit and Darwin; wretched, valiant Dom Pedro who repelled the English and abolished slavery; weary 'Christ-like' Dom Pedro who built a summer palace here, a modest forty-four rooms, and now sleeps his long marble sleep in São Pedro de Alcântara, beside Teresa Cristina, his never-won, never-loved wife. Like others before him and since, he came here, to Petrópolis, where the poets yawn and the night-trees whistle with birds, to escape the sweltering clamor of the coast. For even in summer here the nights are cool, at least generally so, as the air tonight is stifling, draped like a blanket over the hills, the clouds so close, so thick with rain, I feel that I could choke.

Some women have stopped to chat in front of the grocery store below, blunt, heavy-set women with broken-backed sandals and poorly dyed hair who speak of husbands and dish soap with what some nights seems an hysterical longing for truth. I listen now, as I listen each night they appear, studying their gestures, their bloated arms and breasts, and some nights I can hear the insects in their voices (the crickets and spiders), hear the rushing of water, hear the creaking of windows and doors.

Each day with my rum and pencils I peel back a little more of this life, exposing the softer, whiter flesh, each day, each week, that passes but the skin of onions at my feet. Here now, here in Brazil, the minutes, the hours, tick back upon themselves, knitting me a shroud in which each morning I bundle my tired corpse, only to unravel it while I sleep, so that when with a monstrous clatter the boy with the limp raises the grilles on the shop front below I know that I'm dying, *still* dying, not dead. This country of sugar, saints, and slaves, of gauchos, fascists, cannibals, and Jews, this 'land of the future,' this *triste tropique* of kings and queens and dark Candomblé gods is but a billion bright voices, all slurring, all canting, each vying for a place in my head.

And of course there is Zweig himself—Zweig the Mighty, Zweig the Meek: *Today we moved, delighted. The house is tiny, but with a wide covered terrace and a lovely view, quite cool now in winter, and the place is wonderfully deserted, just like Ischl in October or December. Finally somewhere to rest for a few months, and our suitcases will be stored so as not to see them for a long time.*

My book (the story of a life, it seems) is not complete, my work here not yet done. The pages—hundreds of them—have turned their backs on me again, regrouped themselves in strange cabals at my feet, so that some days I cannot find the subject, the thread, but wander blindly through the pages, a rag-and-bone man, a foot-sore gypsy with his *ţambal* and drum.

Nineteen years ago I began this book, *The Life and Flight of Stefan Zweig*, for nineteen long years—more than every year of your life, Yaniv—I have worked to winnow out the wheat of who he was and why anyone, why you, should care, should know, pouring over his letters and diaries and books, walking where he walked, sitting where he sat, reading what he read, dreaming what he dreamt, even laughing at the quips and witticisms that had pleased him so well, yet am up to my knees in chaff.

Now every word, every phrase I write about him, just scatters on the page, refusing its meaning, its place, as though (as if) his own sad life had dispossessed him at last, disowned his very being, (here the dread of us all:) *his ever having been*, had turned its eyes and ears elsewhere, to other people and things, matters with little or no relation to Zweig himself (or distant cousins at best), with whom he rarely spoke and never (or rarely) broke bread, refusing as a story, these pages of mine, to take shape around him, to pro-duce a likeness, a proxy, even a footprint, a shadow—something, *anything*, to bear witness to his bright if haunted life.

Naturally Wensberg, my editor, is furious with me; I received another threat from him today, poor man. He has no idea where I am, though he pesters me with e-mail, aiming high and low, here and there, like a blind man shooting cans. Such is the nature of correspondence these days: one writes from nowhere to nowhere.

For all he can tell, I'm in London or Salzburg or getting drunk in a bar down the street. What is clear is that he is tired of me, tired of this cat and mouse game. He has had enough of my dodging and hedging, and would gladly wash his hands of me, tear up my contract and shred it to bits for the wind, if he didn't *need* to know what has happened to me, if he didn't *need* to know where I am.

In any case it hardly matters now: I've been beaten to the punch. Just this fall a man named Phelps, a writer and scholar I've known for years, a colleague and crony with whom I've often shared a taxi, a meal, published a comprehensive biography of Zweig with a special focus on the final months of his life, here in Petrópolis, in this very house across the street, a time and setting, say the critics, that the author evokes *with a novelist's flair*. The book, some 642 pages (excluding photographs and facsimiles), sold out in less than four months, so that Phelps is now a minor celebrity. In his acknowledgements he was cruel enough to mention my name.

Still I am not discouraged; for better or worse, my book has become something different, something else—the story of Zweig, surely, of Zweig here in Brazil, though he is less the subject proper, it seems, than the lens, the optic, through which I see. Even this, this letter to you, Yaniv, is now a part of his tale. Even Lurdes, Scriabin, the gun in the drawer by my knee. I cannot ignore them, I cannot keep them out. Not Eichmann, not Goethe, not Cheney, not Freud, but they crowd their way in, pushing and shoving, even Bishop and Ovid, my mother, my father, even Mandelstam in Vladivostok has found his way in, so that I am no longer willing to fight it, this other version, this different, froward tale, but follow it where it leads me, no matter *if* or *how badly* it ends. Fear? I have none. Hope? I have plenty. *Even life for evermore.*

I have taken a leave of absence from my teaching in New York, though I will not return. Carla, my department chair, had refused to accept my resignation when I'd tendered it to her, just after the New Year, though I'd cleared out my desk, though I'd sold my apartment and said my goodbyes, badgering me incessantly until I'd agreed to her terms, convinced as she'd been that all I'd needed was a little time away.

She has written me twice since then, once, a week ago, to say hello, to ask about my work, and once, just this morning, to find out how I am, a fretful, rambling, suspiciously unguarded note that has left me feeling muddled all day.

She has never liked me, so much is plain, interrupting me in our weekly meetings, ignoring my e-mail, and never failing to voice her surprise at the popularity of my courses: "Pessoa, Antunes, Saramago? How perfectly bleak of you," she'd reproved me one day, where she'd met me in the street, having for some reason neglected to address me as usual, as 'our own Man Without Qualities,' an epithet she thinks clever, though no one finds it funny anymore. In a fit of caprice, she'd actually mussed my hair where we'd stood waiting for the light, so that from a distance we might have been mistaken for friends. "Adam, Adam," she'd grieved sententiously, only to chuckle to herself and sigh. "Such a cloudy head you have, such a cloudy little head!"

Since then we've generally avoided each other. No doubt she finds me strange. And who can blame her? She wants me to explain.

It was a Friday evening. Late December. It had been snowing all day and I was just finishing up at my desk at work, rereading the final chapters of a dissertation on the obscure Romanian author, Panait Istrati, when I received an e-mail from my uncle, Jack. He rarely ever wrote to me, never really comfortable with the written word, even less so with the computer his wife had bought him as a gift. Just seeing his name on the screen was strange.

He had sent me some photographs he thought I might want to have a look at—such was his simple message to me, the pictures themselves attached as a file.

I was surprised to see that they were photographs of my childhood home. I had not been back to Racine since I was a student in graduate school, since the time I rented a car and made the long drive upstate to help my mother pack up the house for her move to Florida. I had left for boarding school the year my father stopped his car on the tracks, my brother the year thereafter, and had never looked back. Often sentimental about things, I hadn't missed the little town, abandoned there below the highway on a muddy crook of the Susquehanna, indeed had rarely thought of it except vaguely as the place where my mother still lived, isolated by her politics and books as though suspended in some dim, viscous fluid, not stirring, not ageing, at ease before the large river window with her mysteries and crackers and tea.

I'd been happy to think, as I'd approached the town on that occasion, that I would never have to see it again.

Not that anything bad had ever happened to me there. On the contrary, the people had always been kind to me, if a bit wary of my parents who'd kept terriers, listened to classical music, and made the drive to Binghamton three times a week to teach at the university. As the only Jews in town we must have seemed particularly strange to them, not for any pronounced Jewish quality in us (for Jews themselves had often told me we hardly seemed Jewish at all), but because we were clearly *not* Christian, as evidenced each Sunday by our absence at church.

Then there was the matter of our name, Ribeira, hardly Jewish it seemed. Still I'd never sensed any animosity from the adults I knew, from our neighbors, from my teachers, from the parents of my schoolmates and friends, no criticism, no suspicion even, just a curiosity (I sometimes found them staring at me) that as an expression had seemed nothing if not reflexive, benign, so that if as a man I'd had no clear reason for disliking the little town, having when I searched my memory only the gentlest thoughts of it, I'd had even less reason to expect the sudden, violent grief I'd felt at the sight of my uncle's photographs. It was as if I'd been struck a blow. The snow fell, the sky darkened, I'd heard a ringing in my ears and had risen abruptly from my desk, upsetting a pile of books. So acute was my reaction to the photographs that night that it had taken me a few moments to grasp the fact that, after years of blissful silence, in which I'd hesitated to dine in my favorite restaurants, to attend the symphony, or even to listen to the radio, for fear I'd be unable to still the clamor in my head, my tinnitus had returned. No more a roaring in my ears, it was a high, piercing trill accompanied at once by a wave of vertigo and nausea that had swept over me with tremendous violence then was gone.

Slack, bewildered, I'd sat amazed at my desk, uncertain what to think or do, the snow tumbling down outside the window, the past—over which I'd teetered on a wire—suddenly dark and capacious and still.

I'd looked again at the photographs. The old farmhouse had been abandoned; so much was plain. Not a picture, not a stick of furniture remained. The wallpaper in the front hallway was peeling, some of the windows had been broken, there were leaves on the kitchen floor. Had my mother been living I would have called her at once to ask her what she knew, but she'd been dead for years, and in any case had long lost touch with the couple who had purchased the house from her, a retired military man and his schoolteacher wife.

Only my brother, and my uncle himself, remained to remember the house at all, to remember it as I did, for even Aunt Aia was dead, killed of a sudden by a blood clot in her ankle, then replaced, as one might a broken dish, by a woman of the same strange name.

They had found the door to the house ajar. Aia (the second) had taken the photographs, close to three dozen of them, had snapped away at the place with no more knowing than a tourist set loose in the Forum in Rome, so that I'd had to struggle to make sense of what she'd wrought.

My uncle himself had said nothing about the photos, had made no effort to piece them together for me, to remember, explain, though he'd loved the old place, I knew, having enjoyed many a happy holiday with us there. He'd written simply to inform me that the house was to be razed, the property (including the old pump house and barns) having been purchased by the gravel company across the road. He'd thought I might like to see it one last time.

And I had. All night I'd studied the ghostly prints, climbed the old staircase, wandered the void and milky rooms, amazed, aghast, at the images before me on the screen, at their mute, ethereal insistence, a petition, a claim on me, that finally forced me out into the streets, then abandoned to the thickly falling snow. Looking at the photographs, I'd never felt so lonely, so empty, never feared so little, so much. For suddenly, like anger trapped too long beneath the skin, the memories had burst forth in my brain, as if to reclaim that elusive terrain: my mother, gin in hand, laughing, sarcastic; Joseph, my brother, fretting his bottom lip; my father, glasses spattered, adoring, declaiming (Horace or Virgil), grilling hamburgers and chicken and steak.

We'd taken possession of the old farmhouse the year I'd turned ten. My mother had seen an advertisement for the place—the house and barns, the river land below—on one of the bulletin boards at the university in Binghamton where my father had accepted a job at a significant cut in pay, teaching rhetoric and Latin to freshman. He had suffered a nervous breakdown the year before while teaching at Fordham: one night a policeman had found him huddled in a stairwell in Queens.

My father had liked the house at once; it had seemed to calm him—the worn wooden floors, the dark brick fireplaces, the towering elms in the yard. He had liked the smell of the barns, long-abandoned, the bits of straw and feather and dung. Together that first day (my mother and brother had refused to join us) we'd climbed a ladder to the empty loft of the slumping red barn by the house, from where we'd looked out over the brightly stubbled fields to the ribbon of river through the trees.

He'd talked a lot about Indians that year, about the Algonquin, the Oneida, the Iroquois, and the Susquehannock, after whom the wide, shallow river was named, often showing me the arrowheads and sinkers he'd discovered in his evening rambles through the freshly plowed fields. And once he'd taken me to the cemetery above the nearby town of Owego where he'd shown me—for no reason he'd explained—the monument to The Mohawk Maiden, Sa-na-na, who, in the winter of 1852, was crushed to death by a train.

One of the first things he'd done, once we were settled in the house, was to buy himself some tools, some rakes and shovels and hoes. He'd cleared out the ground floor of one of the tumbledown barns, set up a workbench in one of the empty stalls, then hired some locals to install more windows and lights. One day he'd bought himself some overalls and a large straw hat, which soon were soaked through with his sweat, as he ploughed up the earth and planted seeds for a garden out back.

He'd seemed to have forgotten the book he'd been working on, a treatise on Roman sacral poetry, a project that once had filled his waking hours and to which he'd already devoted more than a decade of writing and research. At first a worry to my mother, she'd soon resigned herself to the change in him, to his idle, broken whistling, to the livid color in his normally pallid cheeks, helping him with the watering and weeding, and praising him lavishly for his tomatoes and lettuce, for his carrots and basil and peas.

My father had seemed happy then. Ever meticulous, he'd kept a journal of his new life there, in that house by the river, an annotated ledger in which he'd recorded everything he'd planted that first year: the larches and locusts, the pines (Pitch and Scotch) and maples (Sugar, Silver, Red), the lettuces (Butter Crunch, Oak Leaf, Romaine), the onions (Sweet Spanish, Utah), the beets (Chioggia, Detroit), and the radishes (Amethyst, Red Meat, and D'Avignon), which he'd liked to slice with a knife and eat raw. He'd pruned the many trees and bushes that had overgrown the place. On his little green tractor he'd mown the wide green lawns and, with the help of a neighbor, had painted the red barn white. Sometimes, on the weekends, he'd played poker with friends, men, mostly locals, he'd met at the Nichols Hotel.

It was after that first long summer, when the sky had clouded over, when the plants in the garden had gone to seed, that he'd taken a turn for the worse. He'd still risen early, when for a time he could be found clearing the hillside behind the house, covered, as we'd found it, with a glittering compost of rusted cans and broken glass, or at work down by the river, hacking a path through the trees. Yet by noon each day he'd found himself spent, too exhausted to read or write, too tired even to watch TV, and had either collapsed in his chair by the dining room fireplace or had climbed the steep stairs to his bedroom, from which he hadn't emerged until late that same night, when he would sit in the kitchen and think.

Some mornings, in the course of that first long winter, I'd awakened to find him gone. He'd liked to go for breakfast at a diner by the old courthouse in town where he would eat his eggs and toast before scouring the antique shops along River Row. Fitful, compelled by some reckless new pulse, he'd brought home a baffling variety of things he'd found at a bargain there, in the little shops along the river: cow bells, dough bowls, a sausage grinder, some railroad lanterns (*Armspear*, *St. Lawrence*, and *Dietz*), rusted pulleys, hay hooks, ice tongs, bobbin quills, some wooden hog scrapers, an antique hat stretcher, and a set of large cast iron bees, which we'd used in the summertime to keep the doors from slamming shut.

One day he'd purchased a pair of ladderback chairs with broken cane seats that he'd presented to my mother, where she'd sat playing the piano in the living room, with a guilty, boyish grin. Pushing her glasses to the top of her head, she'd looked at the chairs, she'd looked at my father, then looked at the chairs again, when she'd burst into tears.

Contrite (he was well aware of their debts), he'd been all the more determined to make good on what he'd done. After acquiring the requisite supplies, he'd set up a kerosene heater in the barn, where, in a matter of weeks, and with the help of an old manual he'd found, he'd taught himself the difficult art of caning chairs.

I remember how he'd toiled for hours at a stretch that winter, often late into the night. Sometimes, when he was feeling good, when his progress was steady, he'd invited me to join him there, explaining to me, with a feverish intensity, as I'd shivered there beside him in the barn, how to snip and remove the loops of old cane, while the hank of new cane was soaking. He'd let me hold the pegs he'd used to pin the new strands in place before tying them off, a task to which I'd looked forward in the long, desolate stretches—the days and weeks—when we'd scarcely spoken at all.

It was not until February of that first year that my father had opened up the study my mother had prepared for him, a small, disused room, perhaps originally a sewing room, by the bathroom at the head of the stairs. Furnished with a squat, darkly stained desk, a reading chair and lamp, and an old day bed she'd found in the attic and covered with a cloth, the room had seemed sufficient for his needs.

He'd spent the initial days there just sitting in silence. Occasionally we'd heard him cough; sometimes the door had creaked open then clicked shut again. Then one day the typing had begun, a steady clacking that had settled the mood of the house like the hum of cicadas in June.

From the driveway at night I'd been able to watch him at his desk, pecking away at his typewriter or gazing vacantly at the books on his shelves, one of which he'd occasionally removed to sniff, sometimes leafing through its well-worn pages.

He'd loved the Roman poets—Horace, Catullus, Statius, and Ovid, some of whose verses he'd read aloud to my brother and me when we were young: *Decorum's flung to the wind, a maenadic frenzy grips her, she rushes headlong off after fire and steel... Let us live, my Lesbia, let us love... The wandering wives of the rank he-goats search with impunity through the safe woodland groves for the hidden arbutus and thyme...*

I remember him telling me about Ovid's banishment from his beloved Rome, and about his *Tristia* or 'Lamentations', a collection of letters in elegiac couplets that he'd written in his exile by the Black Sea, lengthy, woebegone missives in which he'd described in fine, nearly clinical detail his wretched state of body and mind, and in which he'd addressed, with love and longing, his grieving wife and the many good friends he'd left behind him there, as well as the emperor himself, from whom, if to no avail, he'd variously begged forgiveness. I'd often pictured him—part Napoleon, part Dreyfus—perched grimly on a rock by the sea.

To please my father I'd studied Latin in high school, though once in college I'd swiftly abandoned it, first for French, then for German and Portuguese, a decision (though by then my father was dead) that had felt like a betrayal of him, of his very heroes themselves, so that as I'd sat looking at the photographs my uncle had sent me that night, the snow tumbling down outside, I'd felt a sadness I hadn't felt in years. More remorse than nostalgia, the feeling had unnerved me. I'd struggled to imagine what I'd done to hurt him, my father, for my sense of guilt, of misgiving, was real.

Again that night I'd seen him standing by the grill out back with his spatula and tongs, heard my mother laughing, felt the warm river light as it streamed up to where we'd trembled beneath the elms, circling us like smoke, then sweeping us gently off our feet. Even my grandmother Margaret was there, with her cut-glass eyes and easy parrot-chuckle, having slipped from beneath her stone by the river to join us on the wide green lawn as if to crown and irradiate the night, one of those vast summer nights that fall so swiftly, so reverently and deep.

The next day, still shaken by the photographs, I'd found I could barely rise from my bed. My head ached, my ears rang; my nausea had returned. I'd assumed I had the flu, had taken aspirin, drunk chicken broth and tea, but my condition had only worsened, so that by the third day I'd fallen into a delirium, a turbid sea of hallucinations and dreams, only to wake the next day, confused and exhausted, the sheets soaked with my urine and sweat.

Oddly I'd dreamt of your mother, Yaniv, though I'd scarcely thought of her in years, but with a bitterness that sometimes marred the edges of sleep. I'd dreamt she'd returned to me like a guardian angel to nurse me back to health. So vivid were the dreams of her, so particular, so lucid their detail, that I can see her even now, beautiful as ever with her sullen grins and sighing, with her blunt-cut hair and haughty, girlish breasts.

I never knew her, your mother, even when I knew her best, when in the mornings full of light and mercy I could smell the coffee on her breath, kiss her eyelids, kiss (if she were sleeping) her elbows and kneecaps and toes. It had been her dream to live in Brazil, she'd often told me, to live drunk like the poet Bishop in a land too beautiful, too wistful to dream.

Trapped together in New York with the rain pouring down, we'd done our best not to surrender too quickly, too soon. My book on Zweig had been going poorly, six people had just been killed in an attack on the World Trade Center, and the city was cold and gray. Your mother had peered over my shoulder and grinned—the empty pages, the grief. She'd bitten me on the ear so that it bled, and for days we hadn't spoken, sullen, reproachful as cats, hadn't even tempted the notion that life was anything more that, anything more than bickering and cigarettes and rain.

It had rained every day for weeks, the drains backed up, the streets thick with muck, great holy rivers of filthy human slush. Some days with the rain on ours heads, with the rain pouring down, she hadn't bother to stir from our bed, smoking and read-ing, muttering verses, curses, so that even the pages I'd written had turned blank, when there'd been nothing left for me to do but read my way back into Zweig's life, turning page after page in book after book—his novels and portraits, his letters and poems and plays—refusing even to look at the newspapers (I could hear the television on), each of them calling the faithful and faithless to death.

Zweig the Mighty, Zweig the Meek: your mother had liked the epithets, though she'd refused to hear about Lotte, the Elysian, anonymous Lotte, Zweig's life-faithful, death-faithful wife. She'd refused to hear another word about his suits and shoes, about his pens and cigars, about his love of music, about the libretto he'd written for Strauss' *Die Schweigsame Frau*. She'd forbidden me at the top of her lungs to ever speak of him again—*that thanatophile, that prig*, to ever mention his flight and exile, his Mary Queen of Scots, his wretched, aching teeth. She was sick of pity, sick of suicide and Jews, though once while it was raining, when the night pressed hard against the windows, when even the bookshelves groaned with the weight of what they knew, she'd let me read aloud to her one of his later poems, while she'd smoked and sighed in our bed:

> More lightly now the passing hours
> Touch the hair that turns to grey
> Only the cup that's nearly drained
> Reveals its floor of gold at last.
> Premonition of approaching night
> Comes not as pain but as release.
> Pure delight of worldly contemplation
> Knows only he who nothing more desires,
> And nothing cares for past success,
> Laments no more things undone,
> And finds that growing old in years
> Is just a gentle way to start to leave.

Never is the prospect clearer
Than in the glow of the departing day,
Never is life more truly loved
Than in the shadow of renunciation.

She hadn't liked it, the poem, not really: another smoke-ring, a puff. It had simply been enough, or not enough to like or dislike, to gut for sacred signs, but enough, just enough not to warrant more (or less), which is the way the world had seemed to me then, when each morning I'd raised the broken blinds to find—tipping on my toes, your mother sulking in the sheets behind me—that the city I'd spun from straw that night was still rooftops and tar pots and rain.

Your mother had begged me not to tell her more about Zweig, about his devoted spaniel, Kaspar, about his friendships with Herzl, Brod, and Freud. She'd begged me not to breathe another word about his first and slighted wife, stopping up her ears and humming hard at me whenever I looked up from my work, as though his life were nothing but the plot of a film that she would someday—she couldn't bear the thought of now—that she would someday like to see. With the rain on her head, with the rain pouring down, she'd quoted Milton at me (*They hand in hand, with wand'ring steps and slow...*), broken my pencils, swept my papers off the desk. A certain look in my eyes had been enough to make her storm from the room in rage. Happy—yes, she was happy that Zweig was dead. Every day she'd cursed the man (and me)—only to conceive of *you*. It's true! She'd already chosen your name: he will prosper: *Yaniv.*

Even that I've included here: the verses, the curses, that shimmering instant she murmured your name. Here in this letter I've recorded—for me, for you, yes, especially for you, Yaniv—the thousand little things your mother cried. For now that she is dead, I want to tell you everything I've felt and seen, everything (what little) I know. For better or worse, I want you to see me as I am, as you must never forgive me, but love your mother, Yaniv, and choke this blessing down. You must swallow it like bone meal and ash. For it is all that I have; all that I can leave you are words… And what is a Jew but words, a skein, a tangle of words?

There is a tradition, dating back to Isaac and his sons, to Jacob and Esau, in which a dying rabbi completes his tenure on earth by writing an ethical will for his congregants, a *tzava'ah*, in which he sets forth for them, for those to survive him, his vision of the world to come, the lessons he has learned, a blueprint of the lives he hopes they will live. For it was the world-worn Jacob, with his guilty dreams of angeled ladders, who'd commanded his sons, "Come together, that I may tell you what is to befall you in the days to come…"

—Such as that, Yaniv, I will not presume to tell you, to know, nor will I call you to my side, call you here, to Petrópolis, to Brazil, but will whisper the words, speak them softly in your ear, so that no matter where you are you might hear them when you will. For like your mother, you need silence and darkness to think. You need to breathe deeply, dream of bright, ineffable things.

That was your mother's trick, you know, what she fed you in the womb. In the months before you were born, she'd eaten nothing that didn't bloom, had slept endlessly, narcotically (*deep-asleep… yet all-awake*), and had begged me to tell her of beautiful things— of seashells and monkeys, of temples and jaguars and kings.

And she'd loved to hear about Brazil. As she'd shivered in our bed with the rain pouring down, I'd told her all about the trees in the jungle here with their bright, alchemical names: *cambucá, sapucaia, grumixama, jabuticaba.* I'd named the world for her, my sullen little Eve—tree by tree, bird by bird, flower by flower of warm Brazilian skin: *Acastanhada* (cashew-like tint), *Alverenta* ('shadow in the water'), *Bem-clara* (parchment-like; translucent), *Bugrezinha-escura* (Indian characteristics), *Burro-quando-foge* ('Burro running away,' implying racial mixture of unknown origin), *Cabocla* (mixture of white, Negro, and Indian), *Cardão* (thistle colored), *Cor-de-cuia* (tea colored; prostitute), *Jambo* (the color of a blood orange), *Lilás* (lily), *Malaia* (from Malabar), *Melada* (honey colored), *Morena-fechada* (very dark, almost mulatta), *Morena-roxa* (purplish tan), *Mulatinha* (lighter-skinned white-Negro), Pálida (pale), *Paraíba* (like the color of marupa wood), *Queimada* (burnt), *Retinta* ('layered' dark skin), *Rosa-queimada* (burnished rose), and *Saraúba* (a complexion like white meringue!).

She'd loved the strange, soft-blooming names, and she'd loved, when lonely, when impatient for you, to hear about Marie Antoinette, anything at all, though it was Zweig and she knew it, *his* Antoinette, all tangled in vines, from which, her favorite part, I read aloud to my landlady, Lurdes, just this morning when she knocked at my door. She too was feeling lonely and heartsick for her son and had asked me to read again the part she too loves best when the child-bride, Marie, soon to be the Dauphiness of France, is escorted amidst a cavalcade of three hundred and forty horses from her childhood home in Vienna through Upper Austria and Bavaria to the imperial border, the Rhine:

After endless deliberations as to whether the formal reception of the bride was to take place upon Austrian or upon French territory,

27

I'd begun aloud to her this morning, the refrigerator humming, the smoke from her cigarette curling up through the bright and clammy air, *After endless deliberations...a cunning man among them hit upon the Solomonic expedient of choosing for this purpose one of the small uninhabited sandbanks in the Rhine, between France and Germany, and therefore in no-man's land. Here was to be erected a wooden pavilion for the ceremonial transference—a miracle of neutrality. There were to be two anterooms looking towards the right bank of the Rhine, through which Marie Antoinette would pass as Archduchess—and two anterooms looking towards the left bank of the Rhine, which she would traverse as Dauphiness of France after the ceremony. Between them would be the great hall in which the Archduchess would be definitively metamorphosed into the heiress to the throne of France. Costly tapestries from the archiepiscopal palace concealed the wooden planking; the University of Strasbourg lent a baldachin; and the wealthy burghers of Strasbourg were glad to have their finest articles of furniture hallowed by close contact with royalty. It need hardly be said that no one of middle-class origin was really entitled to set eyes upon the interior of this sanctum of princely splendour, but its guardians (as is usual in such cases) were open to corruption by a liberal tip, and so, a few days before Marie Antoinette's arrival, some German students, spurred on by curiosity, made their way into the half-finished room. One of these youths, not long past his teens, a tall fellow, with an eager expression and with the stamp of genius upon his virile brow, could not feast his eyes enough on the gobelin hangings, whose themes had been taken from Raphael's cartoons. In Strasbourg cathedral he had just had a revelation of the glories of Gothic architecture, and was ready to show no less appreciation, no less love, for classical art. Filled with enthusiasm, he was explaining to his less well-informed comrades the significance of the beauties unexpectedly revealed to him by the Italian master—but suddenly the flow of his eloquence ceased, he showed disquiet and knitted his dark eyebrows with something akin to anger. He had just realized what the design on the tapestries represented—a myth that was certainly unsuitable as setting for a wedding festival—the tale of Jason, Medea and Creusa, the crowning example of an unhappy marriage. 'What,' exclaimed the talented youngster, ignoring the astonishment of the bystanders, 'is it permissible thus unreflectingly to display before the eyes of a young queen entering upon married life this example of the most horrible wedding that perhaps ever took place? Among the French architects, decorators and upholsterers, are there none who can understand that pictures mean something, that pictures work upon the senses and the feelings, that they effect impressions, that they arouse ominous intimations? It seems to me as if a hideous spectre had been sent to greet this lady at the frontier; this lady who is, we are told, beautiful, and full of the joy of life!' His friends found it difficult to assuage his anger, and had almost to use force before they could make Goethe (for this was the student's name) leave the wooden reception house. But when, not many hours later, the members of the marriage train, glad at heart, and engaged in cheerful conversation, entered the gaily decorated building, not one of them was aware that the prophetic eyes of a great poet had already glimpsed the black thread of doom interwoven into the brightly coloured hangings. The handing-over of Marie Antoinette was to signify her farewell to all the persons and all the things which linked her with the House of Hapsburg. The masters of the ceremonies had devised a peculiar symbol of this change of mental and material habitat. Not only had it been decreed that none of the members of the Austrian train were to accompany her across the invisible frontier line, but the sometime archduchess was, on entering France, to have discarded every stitch of her native attire, was not to wear so much as shoes or stockings or shift that had been made by Viennese artificers. From the moment when she became Dauphiness of France, all her wrappings and trappings were to be of French origin. In the Austrian antechamber, therefore, in the presence of her Austrian followers, this girl of fourteen had to strip to the buff. Naked as on the day she was born, the still undeveloped girl disclosed her slender body in the curtained chamber. Then she was quickly redressed in a chemise of French silk, petticoats from Paris, stockings from Lyons, shoes made by the shoemaker to the French court, French lace. Nothing was she to keep that might be endeared to her memory, not a ring, not a cross—for it would be a grave breach of etiquette were she to retain so much as a buckle, a clasp or a favorite bracelet—and from this same moment she was to part company with all the familiar faces. Can we be surprised to learn that the poor child, overwhelmed by so much ceremonial and hurled (the word is not too strong) into a foreign environment, should have burst into tears?*

And there I'd concluded the scene for Lurdes this morning, when she'd sniffled her thanks to me, then gobbled the last of her rum.

Now the bottle of *Divininha* is almost empty and I pour what remains in my glass, adding a squeeze of lime juice and some ice. The first sip is always the best, tightening the muscles in my jaw. I drink it down and groan, for time here has stopped, the insolent clock. Fretful, impatient, I am tempted to step out for more cigarettes, which I often buy in the market downstairs or in the restaurant across the street where the pretty young albino sits all day behind the bar with a baby at her breast. I'd like to see her, this Senda, this simple sanguine saint; I'd like to speak to the curious features of her face: the mannish chin, the twisted lip, the eyes without ripples or rims. And I'd like to hear her sing, as I've heard her sing before, for my sadness has returned today, climbed the stairs and let itself in at my door. Perched like a crone in its high-backed chair, it gestures at me with its fine and airy hands, forbidding me favors, forbidding me breath, only to prattle like a schoolmarm: "…for the moment/No love or the other thing…"—some lines, once sung by your mother, from some lines by Mina Loy:

> for the moment
> No love or the other thing
> Only the impact of lighted bodies
> Knocking sparks off each other
> In chaos

This sadness is many things: pens in a drawer, spots on a wall, some people playing cards—your mother, my father (no ace up his sleeve), my brother and mother still bickering themselves to grief. Sadness, my cicerone; it met me at the airport this time, carried my suitcase, sat beside me on the bus.

For all my trips to Brazil I'd scarcely known Rio at all, having usually made my way straight here, to Petrópolis, never caring to see the sights, to taunt the old lions as gods and tourists do, so that what could I say when my sadness balked, when it signaled the driver then led me by the hand to another bus, a different bus with a different driver and fare?

I'd followed it throughout the city that day, to Centro, Zona Norte, and Zona Sul, from the crowded beaches of Leme and Ipanema to the heights of Páo du Açucár. Together we'd climbed our way through the dark *favelas* where the children threw sticks at me and the pop-eyed old women spat blood.

At one point it had stopped, my sadness, pointed to a curb where a little boy had been struck dead by a bus that morning, only to guide me by the hand to a small cafe with peeling blue walls where a woman sat weeping beneath a poster of a bull. She'd just smothered her dog, my sadness had explained to me: the dog had been ill and she'd smothered it to save it from pain, though now she couldn't bring herself to return to the apartment, to mount the stairs. She couldn't stop herself from crying.

At that my sadness had smiled wistfully, then shrugged its shoulders, as if ready to release me at last, to return me to the bus where it had found me with my suitcase and sighing, when it took me by the hand once more, pausing briefly before the building in which Saramago's lonely doctor had run his lonely practice, only to lead me off along a chain of narrow lanes to a little park, somewhere deep in the city, Praça São Salvador, where the pigeons cooed glumly and seaweed hung like tinsel from the trees, to tell me in a hideous whisper that our dear old friend Zweig was dead.

Only then did I recognize the hand on my arm, the wrist-watch, the beard, only then did I recognize Phelps, my long-time rival, sitting there beside me on the bench, legs crossed, belching softly to himself. Only then did I grasp what he meant and think to seize him by the throat, to dash out his brains on the cobblestones there where the children turned circles on their bikes, knowing full well that I wouldn't, I couldn't, that I was helpless to resist him now, this man, this scholar, who had swallowed Zweig whole, had ingested and digested him, and now picked his teeth beside me in the sun, the bits of tendon, the meat, who, as if to drive the point home, to show me the scraps on his plate, pressed me on through the city that day, through the warm, milky rain, and up the wide, garish steps of the Museau da República, through a gaggle of schoolgirls, premature saints with their lip gloss and gum, to the lavish third-floor bedroom where the former president and dictator, Getúlio Vargas, (there the pistol, there his unmade bed) had shot himself one high bright morning, a bullet to the chest.

And now no rain, no saints at all. Not a drizzle, a drop, though it's pouring there in Haifa, I see. I can see it on the map. Every day I look up the weather there, check the forecast the instant I rise.

I like to think of it raining there, of it raining there at night. I picture you reading in your room, watching a soccer match with your step-father or talking with some dark-eyed girl on the phone.

Some days, having searched your address on the internet, I sit staring at the satellite image of your house, turning it this way and that, moving up and down your street, wondering what it would be like to be standing there in the flesh before your house, before the wide turquoise gate, smelling the rain in the trees, hearing the rise and fall of your voices inside. I imagine opening the gate, latching it behind me, even making a fist here to knock on your door. I try never to think of you lonely.

This here is the building where I live. I took the photo myself, just yesterday. See the woman in the window there? That's Lurdes,

my landlady. My window is just to the right of hers, the window
of my bedroom and study. It's where I'm sitting right now.

I found the apartment by chance, the last time I was here. I'd
stopped in at the little market downstairs to get something to drink
when I'd overheard a woman telling the cashier that she was looking for a short-term tenant for her brother's apartment upstairs. Of
course it was Lurdes, before I knew her and could think about her
name. She was complaining about her brother, *porco preguiçoso*,
about how he expected her to do everything for him while he was
away: dust his rooms, pay his bills, and tend his 'bloody' orchids,
suas orquídeas malditos. For weeks he hadn't even called.

Parcels in hand, she'd thanked God for me (Imagine my appear-
ing like that!), then cursed the broken elevator, when together we'd
climbed the dimly lit stairs at the back, the landings of which were
littered with cigarette butts and spotted in places by mold (which

flourishes here, no matter the scrubbing, the bleach), mounting flight after huffing flight to her own small apartment near the end of the hall, where she'd left the television on, her battered blue door ajar.

She never kept rum in the house, she'd declared to me forthwith, not bothering to unpack her groceries, but leading me straight through to the living room, cluttered with dark, heavy furniture, pictures of saints, stacks of lurid-looking detective novels, and an assortment of garish Chinese knickknacks (dragons and Foo dogs and fat laughing Buddhas), where the television blared and her tiny piebald dog sniffed the tips of my shoes. No, not a drop since her husband died, drank himself to death, she'd explained to me without feeling, only to ask me, before I'd even seen her brother's apartment, if she could keep a small bottle with me. About rum, she'd attested gravely, she was deeply superstitious.

"So what *do* you think about?" she'd inquired at length, once she'd settled herself in her chair between the windows. In the market downstairs she had asked me what I did for a living, a question to which, feeling flippant, I'd replied, "I think."

"You *think?*"

"I mean, I write. I'm a writer," I'd explained to her at once, but she'd paid me no mind, cackling loudly and throwing up her hands.

"*Um pensador!*" she'd repeated for the buxom cashier, and for those in line behind her. *"Pense num pensador!"*

"Well, go on now," she'd pressed me cocking her head where I sat before her on the couch. "Tell me what you think about."

"Why, I think about lots of things..." I'd hedged, patting her ugly dog in my lap. It had a curious, yeast-like smell.

"What sort of things?"

"Oh, I don't know...about people mostly. I think a lot about people. You know, who they were and how they got that way. That kind of thing..." I'd added vaguely, for she'd suddenly lost interest in me, it was plain, rummaging around in her purse until she'd found her receipt from the market downstairs, which she'd quickly examined before exclaiming, "Of course! I knew it! She charged me full price!"

But for a few stock questions about New York, and about my surname, Riberia, about which I'd had nothing intriguing to say, she'd expressed little interest in me that first day, hardly curious about who I was, about what I was doing here, about how it was I knew this language of hers, knew by head, by heart, the works of Gonçalves Dias and Camões, some of which I'd recited like a schoolboy to please her.

Still, she'd seemed satisfied with me—with my appearance, my manner, and with my Portuguese, which she'd sifted like flour as I spoke, smiling at this word, frowning at that, while never doubting I was right for the place, that I would pay the rent in cash, mind her brother's orchids, and vanish in a flash if he returned.

She'd made me lemonade from a can that morning and together we'd smoked and talked and rummaged through the catalogues piled high beside her chair to find a gift for her niece, one Dulce Maria, who was soon to be confirmed, pretty dresses and shoes, while the war in Iraq flickered manically beside her. *Forty people were killed and more than a hundred wounded in Baghdad yesterday in a day of sectarian violence that experts fear will spread quickly throughout the country.* Humvees, wailing mothers, the blackened shell of a car. Cheney had appeared with his smirk, when the highlights of a soccer match had flashed across the screen.

Hot, restless, I'd been eager to see her brother's apartment, positioned as it was—as by some miraculous twist of fate—directly across the street from Zweig's old house, a fact to which Lurdes herself had seemed indifferent, when I'd explained it to her, chattering on to me about the plumbing and about her taxes as though she hadn't spoken with anyone in days. She'd told me all about the tenants in the building, whom she'd named for me one-by-one, describing their particular histories (the deaths and divorces and disappointments) with an affection for detail that left me speechless and numb, only to guide me through an album of family photographs—mostly of her late husband and her son, though there were two of her mother as a child in Macao, a pretty girl with long hair, finally playing for me some of her favorite records, those of Tito Schipa, Mercedes Sosa, and Carlos Gardel, her eyes tearing up at the latter's rendition of 'El Día Que Me Quieras'.

Reluctant even then to let me go, to show me her brother's apartment, she'd prepared for me a plate of scrambled eggs and sliced papaya, which I'd washed down, beneath a cage of canaries, with a bottle of ice-cold beer. There, as I'd dutifully eaten the eggs and the papaya, as I'd dutifully swallowed the beer, she'd passed the time by reading aloud to me from the latest edition of *Diário*, the popular local paper, as a means of acquainting me with the town itself, and its people, of which she was both critical and proud, occasionally fanning herself with the sports section and stopping now and then to flesh out some comment or allusion that only a local could know.

Now Lurdes is banging her pots and pans; I can hear her through the wall. Surely she must wonder about me, about my work, my habits, about the various sounds I make. She must wonder what it is I do at night; she must wonder where I go.

Some days when she visits me in her housedress and slippers, to feel my forehead and to change my sheets, I watch her examining the familiar rooms, dropping ashes on my books and papers (some of which I suspect she has read), while opening the cabinets and drawers, the shims and braces of which swell like tumors when it rains, only to conclude her inspection by testing the potting material of each of her brother's many orchids, his fussy blend of coco husks, charcoal, and moss. On some such days I see the questions forming themselves in her eyes.

Yet with her first taste of rum her expression clears, her face naked and faithful as a child's. In truth she doesn't want to know anything that might ruffle the gentle waters of her life here. She aspires to nothing, it seems, dreams of nothing but what the days themselves attest: here the sun; a sale on lemons; close the windows before it rains.

One morning I taught her how to play chess and now she plays it with a vengeance. She often takes minutes to make her moves, muttering, sighing, adjusting the spotted kerchief she wears on her blunt and dimpled head. She is a woman of cryptic signs and sorrows, a wellspring of oaths and imprecations that pop and fizzle about her like some carbonated aura of life.

Once, when we were playing, when I was thinking about Zweig, when I was thinking about Zweig and chess and waiting for Lurdes to make her next move, I'd asked her if she'd ever heard of the man, the subject of my book.

"You mean, the house across the street? He killed his wife there. Murdered her in her sleep."

"No, no," I'd protested, "they were very much in love. They died in each other's arms."

But Lurdes would have none of it. "He was a Nazi and killed her, everyone knows. She was Jewish, a girl half his age, and now the house is cursed."

Hers was by no means the first confabulation I'd heard about Zweig and his house. One old man had insisted to me, where we'd sat together in the bar across the street, that Zweig had hidden his diamonds there on the property, gems he'd smuggled out of Europe before the war. Kids sometimes dug up the garden at night. He'd sworn to me—crossing himself, hand on heart—that now the diamonds lay buried in Zweig's own grave.

Of course there is little truth in what they say, though I can hardly fault them for such tales, for their desire—no matter how puerile, how crass—to fathom the presence of this urbane, world-famous writer who'd appeared here like a god one day, with his wife and luggage, as out of the clear blue sky. They can hardly be blamed for crimping the facts, for pausing on the sidewalk before the overgrown house, as I've often seen them do, stopping as if in disgrace before a church or temple, as if in amazement, in shame, before some ancient pagan shrine, making a show of adjusting their parcels, their dresses, their hats, while glancing up at the house within which they sense something awful, something tragic, occurred, appraising it all, the sagging veranda, the stubborn ivy, the darkened windows with their rusted white grilles, as if half-expecting Zweig himself to emerge through the door and confront them where they stand. For even now the place suggests him, his life, his death; even now it draws one up, compels one to wonder, to think.

The original steps from the street to the house are gone, as are most of the hydrangeas, torn up, replaced some years ago by a short driveway and a small garage. There were fifty of them when Zweig lived here, exactly fifty steps, when, freshly bathed and dressed in one of his pale, summer-weight suits, he'd descended the staircase each morning through a sea of hydrangeas and crossed the busy road to *Café Elegante* (on the site where my building now stands) for a cup of sweet dark coffee before commencing his work. There, surrounded by local workmen, he'd liked to amuse the kindly proprietor with his Charlie Chaplin and his fits of Portuguese. For he'd never stopped trying, Zweig; he'd known that this was it, Brazil, his last and third life, that there was nowhere left to turn.

See him for yourself there where he stands by the door. Smiling, uneasy, he takes a measure of the dark, roughly planked room, appraising the pictures on the wall, the broom by the kitchen, the half a dozen tables crowded with silent mule drivers slurping their coffee and chewing their day-old bread. As usual he has brought with him his copy of the morning paper, which, once seated, he unrolls before him like a parchment, a scroll, perusing the crudely printed articles with a grin and a sniff. When at last the owner appears with his coffee they shake hands, chuckle fatly as friends.

Zweig is full of jokes this morning, pitching his voice just high enough so that everyone in the room can hear him. He tells the one about the man and the clam, then the one about the woman with her talking blue hat, when for a time he and the owner grumble theatrically over the news in the paper—a farce and set-piece, some dreadful, some hopeful, burlesque.

Now in walks Spengler again: Is there a logic to history? he demands of me and of Zweig, who—caught forks in hand in the middle of performing a roll dance for the delighted proprietor—looks at me aghast. A logic to history? I realize it is a question I've been trying to answer for years, ever since I started this book on Zweig.

The summer you were born, Yaniv, I was hospitalized for the second time in my life. Nervous exhaustion was your mother's diagnosis; *nerves*, she'd whispered to her family and friends. That year—the blackest I remember—she'd sued me for divorce.

I'd been driving myself hard at work, teaching classes, doing research, speaking at conferences, and trying in vain to get a handle on Zweig, for the more I'd read about him, the more I'd spelled out his life, the more elusive, more improbable he'd seemed. There was plenty to say about the man; rare for writers, he was a celebrity at heart, perhaps the most public writer of his day. No Euripides, he'd left reams of material with which to work. Still my thinking about him had refused to coalesce. Nothing I wrote rang true, so that for months I'd seethed in darkness, smoking and drinking and generally abusing your mother until—broken herself and crying— she'd left me, your mother, for good.

Of course Spengler's a fool, a fop in motley who should have written novels instead. No self-respecting historian would ever read him now, but for a wink at his expense. A logic to history! The minstrel, the clown! What did he know about history, with his quaint morphology and botanical figures of speech, with his Dread and Longing, his Destiny and Incident, his 'thing-becoming' and 'thing-become'? Why, he'd never even heard of 9/11, the State of Israel or the war in Vietnam? Compare Stalin's mustache to a pair of laughing cockroaches? He could never have thought of that!

But I'm getting ahead of myself: too much, too fast.

Who then was this Zweig, you say? A realist, an idealist? A hero, a coward, a fool?

See this photo here? This is not Zweig but a contemporary of his, a Russian-born Jewish writer named David Vogel (You know, *By indirections find directions out...*). He was the subject of my first book. Eager for tenure, having abandoned my Zweig, I'd written a short study of the man, the year you were born, an obituary of sorts, hammered it out on my old Olivetti in less than five months while living alone in a small seaport on the Oregon coast where a friend of mine had a house.

It had rained all winter there, a cold, drizzling rain for which I'd been grateful, hunkering down at the kitchen table for hours each day, and rarely venturing outside but to stagger down the hill a few times a week to buy groceries and to eat fresh crab in one of the only restaurants still open. I'd found mostly locals there, behind the fogged up windows: fishermen, families, the young postman who'd delivered my mail, none of whom had paid me the slightest attention, as I'd gulped down my food and guzzled my beer, though I'd liked to listen to them, when they were not too busy eating, they who knew nothing of my world—of you, of Zweig, of my recent divorce. It had mattered nothing to them whether I lived or died. Even politics and history, about which they'd sometimes argued in jest, seemed to touch them only lightly there, like a lunar landing, like the latest findings on eggs or red meat, so that in all that salt and sea air it wasn't long before I'd achieved a clarity and confidence in my writing (what at times had seemed a veritable *omniscience*) that I've been chasing like a whisper ever since. I'd had only to look at the page in the typewriter for the words to appear, good, lean words, like nails in a plank, like rivets in a plate of steel. It was that easy, the writing, so that I could watch television or listen to the radio without fear of disruption. I could nap when I chose to, the telephone could ring all day, I didn't care, I'd scarcely heard it at all. I could even have a beer with my lunch without troubling my muse. And if I woke at dawn, as I frequently had, standing with my coffee at the living room widow (from which I'd liked to look down upon the old boatyard with its rusted winches and heaps of old netting, and out across the harbor to the distant bay bridge, its arches lost in fog), I could watch the sluggish old trawlers plying their way out through the long rocky channel to the sea without the slightest fear of starting up again, of recommencing my work.

It was there in that lonely seaport that I'd completed my study of Vogel, a spare, strictly academic treatment of his little-known life and work that was picked up by Oxford that same year and published to brief, if critical acclaim. Not even my colleagues had heard of him. Now the book is out of print. Even used copies are difficult to find.

Like Zweig, Vogel had loved Vienna, the music, the theatre, the cafes. He'd done what Jews there did best: he'd talked and listened and read the daily papers. Born in the town of Satanov, in the heart of the Russian Pale, he'd moved to Vienna in 1912, where briefly he'd made a living teaching Hebrew and copying letters for the newly chartered Zionist Federation before being interned as an enemy during the First World War. Once released, he'd promptly married, eventually making his way to Paris with his tubercular young wife, Ilka, who'd died soon after their arrival.

There, stirred by the vibrant city, he'd written poetry and prose, mostly forgettable stuff, before marrying again and moving to Palestine to join the settlers in Jaffa, only to return to France, to Lyon, near the outbreak of WWII, where he was arrested by the Gestapo, deported to Auschwitz, and murdered without a trace.

Yet oblivion proved kinder than Hitler. Some of Vogel's diaries and poems appeared in Israel; he was the subject of a scholarly paper in Rennes; one summer the University of Stuttgart hosted a small colloquium on his work. Then for years he'd disappeared again, so that I'd only learned of him by chance one day while browsing in a bookshop in Greenwich Village. In one of the sidewalk bins on St. Mark's Place, I'd found a novel of his, a tattered paperback called *Married Life*, first published in Palestine in 1929 under the title, *Chai Nissuim*. I'd bought it for a dollar that day.

Married Life tells the story of a poor Jewish intellectual, living hand-to-mouth in 1920's Vienna, who is drawn into a disastrous marriage with an impoverished, sadistic, and deeply anti-Semitic baroness named Thea von Takov. At heart an allegory of Vienna's historical relationship with Jews, it is also Zweig's story, that is, but for the fact Zweig was rich and sated and only married Jews.

At one point, while watching a team of virile young workers loading crates onto a wagon, the novel's protagonist, Rudolph Gurdweill, "glanced contemptuously at his thin, short body, which seemed to him to be made of nerves and brains alone." That too was Zweig: the brainy, anxious, weakling Jew.

Yet it is Vogel's largely incidental descriptions of the cultural life of pre-war Vienna, with its popular theatres and cafes, with its Strauss and Hofmannsthal, its Buber, Lang, and Freud, that are part of the key to understanding Zweig—his grief, his flight, his death by suicide in this remote Brazilian town.

I check the clock on the wall. Eager for a cigarette, I rifle through the drawers of the little desk here, hoping to find a pack, when I am distracted by the handsome, now-familiar Gallimard edition of nude sketches by Gustav Klimt on the shelf beside the bed. It is a lovely book, thick creamy pages, cleanly rendered lines.

Lurdes' brother is an avid book collector—art, philosophy, psychology, history, ornithology, poetry, semiotics, and fiction. His books line the walls of his bedroom here in strictly serried ranks, some of them in German, most of them in Portuguese, English, and French. He never lends them, it is clear, so that as ever I am reluctant to touch them, so perfect are their covers, so flawless their bindings and pages.

The drawings in the volume are impulsive, spare. They are studies, diversions meant to titillate, keyhole musings on the sexual lives of women that strike me, each time I look at them, as decidedly more wishful than true. Still they are not without their beauty, a certain mawkish, Viennese grace. Indeed they reek of the age—the license and dissipation, those 'blurs and smudges' by which the city was then known.

For by then, by the late 1920's, the Hapsburg Empire was at an end, though no one would say it, least of all Zweig, who like so many Jews in Vienna at the time, mistook the end for something new. Hitler—monster that he was—had only delivered the final blow. Yet Vogel had seen it coming, as had Kraus and Freud, as Werfel, Musil, and Roth, all of whom had fled that 'unbreathable air.' Only Zweig had missed it or denied it by holding his breath, by covering his ears and eyes. Only Zweig had tarried there still, hoping for the best, praying each night, with the mystic fervor of a child, that he would wake one morning to learn that the Nazis had vanished, that Hitler, *der Führer*, was dead. For—and here's the difference, you see—Zweig had staked his soul on the future of Europe, on the promise it had made him as a loyal, successful, *acculturated* Jew.

Now picture him here in Petrópolis, in Brazil. Picture him, this celebrated writer, this lover of Beethoven and Goethe, this cosmopolitan dandy with his Savile Row suits and spat-style shoes. Picture him strolling the broken cobblestones, see him chatting gaily with the local mule drivers, whom he meets along the way, see him pause before the quaint, Bohemian-style houses near the center of town as before some sentimental painting of home. Then picture him pushing his way through thick jungle creepers, spattered to the knees with mud.

Living here he'd often complained of the rain, which falls for days on end in the summer season, pouring from the sky until the streams and rivers overflow their banks and the earth is so sodden that the streets are littered with worms. He'd done his best, while the Nazis ran roughshod over Europe, murdering and plundering as they went, to stick to his routine, that strict if simple regimen of reading and writing that had made him his fortune, his name, eager as he was to finish the autobiography he'd started in Ossining and determined to complete his book on Balzac, the manuscript of which had finally arrived from safekeeping in Bath, while still reluctant—it gave him nightmares to think of it—to neglect his daily correspondence, the letters he wrote with little hope of receipt or reply. For in their five short months in the house across the way here they'd seen the steady stream of greetings and good wishes from Europe dwindle suddenly, precipitously, a mouth gaping wide, so that by the end, by the time they'd written their farewell letters, swallowed their pills (first he then she), and climbed into one of the hard, narrow beds together to await the gentle end, they'd been forced to call themselves lucky if they'd received any word from their friends and family at all.

It was the waiting that had frayed their tempers, their nerves. Yet what could they do, they had to keep busy: Lotte with her *Linzertorte* and *Shinkenknödel*, with the cook and maid and gardener, Zweig with his teeth and translations, Zweig with his wretched Portuguese.

Each day, after a morning of reading and writing, he'd walked to exhaust himself, charting every street and alley in the town, venturing far and wide, wherever his legs would take him, so that there was scarcely an inch of the old Duas Portas neighborhood—a shop, a doorstep, a cat—he didn't know by heart. Some days he'd walked until he felt he would collapse from the effort, the heat, only to sit sullenly on the covered veranda in his moldy-smelling clothes, while the maid and 'cook-general' prepared their lunch for them, their potted meat and potatoes, their manioc and beans, singing coarsely some love song while rinsing the empty tins.

When not writing or walking, when not tossing and turning

in bed, he'd read his Erasmus or Montaigne in his favorite canvas chair or sat perspiring at his writing table on the veranda, phrasebook and dictionary in hand, working his way through the front page articles of the *Correio da Manhã*, their only real news of the world.

Yet it wasn't easy. By then, by the afternoon each day, it was everything he could do to keep from drowsing, from simply capitulating to the torpor, the heat, where he sat sweating in his shirtsleeves and tie, gazing down upon the narrow, glaucous valley, there beyond the *inga* trees and palms, his mind inert, his limbs like putty, like lead.

For all his diligence (he knew it was the little lapses that unmade one), he'd soon grown tired of the work, the routine, lonely, overwhelmed by the climate, by the dense, nearly hostile beauty of the land, that clamoring, indecipherable riot that rose around him like a pall where he sat. And he was frustrated by his lack of access to good music and books. Despite his initial desire for a little peace and quiet, for some *dolce far niente*, as he'd often praised it to his friends, he'd come to dread the solitude, the dampness. His wife's asthma had exhausted him, her wheezing and coughing, her anxious pacing at night, so that he'd often dreamt of his times alone in London, crisp, capacious days when he'd idled for hours at the National Gallery, gazing at the Memlings and Van Eycks, and in the British Library, where he'd liked to read and write, where he'd often sat, glass in hand, enraptured by Denyer's moth and butterfly paintings or happily perusing the letters and Notebook of his hero, the poet-artist, William Blake. And he'd loved the time he'd spent in Hyde park with its flocks of sheep, its riders and rowers, and its beamish bands of the faithful—the men, women, and children who'd gathered there each Sunday to sing.

He'd missed it all, though he'd never warmed to the English themselves. He'd hated their tea, their pubs, their food. He'd hated their archness, their reserve.

It was the culture itself he'd loved and missed, the genius in the very air one breathed.

Yet what right had he to complain? he'd chided himself each time. The weather in Brazil was clement, the food plentiful, the people honest, descent, and true. What's more, he was healthy, secure. After years of running he could finally catch his breath.

And still he'd fretted the hours each day. *If only... If just...*

When not reading or writing, when exhausted from walking, he'd liked to play chess, to study the master games, and for a time it had sufficed to divert him, but it wasn't long before he'd chafed at the idleness of it, before he'd dreaded the daily games with Lotte on the wide covered terrace where they'd often sat for hours gaping numbly at the rain.

Hope sprang eternal each morning with the postman's appearance at the bottom of the steep flight of steps. Each morning the sky cleared, the leaves glistened, the world was born anew. A single letter—read and discussed and reread—was enough to sustain them for days. Yet most mornings the postman had nothing to give them, didn't even bother to climb the steps, only waved at their faces from the street, when they would retreat to their separate rooms, and again the rain would fall, crashing like cymbals through the trees.

Now the rains here are long overdue. Each day the locals peer up at the sky, shake their heads, and frown. Each day they fondle the brittle leaves of the bushes and trees that overhang the busy street, sniffing their fingers for clues.

Lurdes has a theory about the rains. Once over breakfast she'd told me about the failing coffee crop in Brazil, had insisted to me that each year the rain here fell in direct proportion to the daily consumption of coffee in Italy and France: the more coffee consumed there the less the rain fell here! She'd urged me to check it for myself.

Reluctant to offend her, I'd merely nodded my head, for she is by no means an unintelligent woman, often arriving at the truth (or some such semblance of it) by the most extravagant and mysterious means. It is a theory, no matter how ridiculous, that has gotten under my skin: each day it doesn't rain I see a Frenchman drinking coffee! Such is her effect on me these days that I no longer even try to resist her, but eat her food as I can, listen patiently to her tales about her son, and smile at her weakness for *cachaça*, the sugar cane liquor she calls *abre-coração*.

To pass the time, I've replaced the book on Klimt with another, a thick, leather-bound edition of the poetry of Vallejo, a love-tome of ciphers, of codes, when the telephone rings, a hard jangly old-fashioned ring that reminds me, each time I hear it, of telephones in empty rooms all over the world—in Antwerp and Paris, in Belfast, Bangkok, and Rome.

Even before lifting the receiver I know it is Dario, one of Fernão's former lovers, a younger man, by his voice and temper, who lives with his mother and brothers in Rio, in the sprawling *favela* called Rocinha, where, when not drunk or playing soccer, he drives a taxi for his aunt. So much have I learned—and more.

He begins, as always, by asking to speak to Fernão. I like his voice, the pulse and feathers in it; I like his initial shyness, his restraint, and try to picture the busy shop in which he stands, the shop from which he has placed this and every call since I arrived. For it *is* a shop, I know: I can distinguish the voices, the clinking of bottles, the blare of horns from the street. Softly, through it all, come the usual strains of samba from a radio nearby: *Mas se ela voltar, se ela voltar,/Que coisa linda, que coisa louca…*

When he hears my voice this time he groans, curses me foully, then hangs up the phone.

Once he threatened to kill me, to stab me in the throat (in the throat, *na garganta,* he said). He threatened to drive here from Rio and shoot me dead in the street. And he has promised to kill Fernão, once he returns, to douse his apartment with gasoline and burn the whole building to the ground, for despite what I've told him, poor boy, he's convinced I've taken his place.

—If I loved you… what then?

After the first few times I'd spoken with him, after I'd listened to at least a dozen of his messages on Fernão's old machine, I'd searched the apartment, the cupboards and drawers, for any clue to who he was, this Duke of Illyria, this Brazilian Pierrot, any photos or letters that might render him more clearly to me, but found no trace of him at all.

What is interesting is that there are not only no photos of Dario in the apartment (or of any of Fernão's other friends or lovers, not even of the man he lives with in Paris, a sculptor and painter from Detroit), but there is not a single photo of Fernão himself, not a snapshot, driver's license or old passport to be found. The only photograph I have seen of him, the only image I have from which to conjure this man in whose apartment I've been living for weeks, is a framed photograph of him as a chubby little boy on the back of a pony, taken when he was perhaps five and six, which I'd discovered by chance one day while helping his sister flip the mattress in her room.

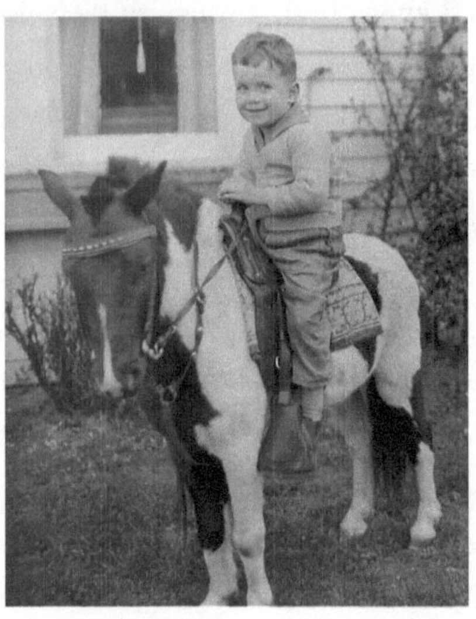

If he is fat now, if indeed he is obese, as his sister Lurdes claims, as his sister Lurdes insists, if he is somehow deformed or otherwise grossly, vulgarly made, there is no way for me to know it, to tell. For almost as if teasing me he has taken all of his clothes with him to France, so that not a shirt, a belt, a pair of trousers, not even a bracelet or ring of his remains behind here from which to extrapolate his size.

Yet I really don't care; I've come to like the quiet mystery of it all, the rare orchids, the artwork, the handsome, well-bound books, so that often, when I've finished my work or am simply unwilling or unable to begin, I wander about the small apartment, squatting, sniffing, getting down on my hands and knees—less the detective than a child in a toy store or zoo.

His taste in art is eclectic, expensive. Included in his small collection are a small stone Jizō, some framed antique maps (Friesland, Barbados, Ceylon), a pair of French cabinet plates of Napoleon and Josephine, a reproduction of a painting of the Chimborazo volcano by Alexander Humboldt, a Tibetan tanka (the wheel of life), and, holding pride of place over the coffee table in the living room, a red Murano chandelier, to which island I myself once paid a visit while in Venice one year to see the Church of Santa Maria e San Donato where it is said the bones of the dragon slain by Saint Donatus lie buried.

And there is much Brazilian art, too, from prints and paintings to gilded wood saints to a rustic assortment of tiny metal charms—hearts and legs and breasts. On the wall by the front door hangs a wooden bullroarer with a faded fish design, which, when spun at the end of a cord (so I've learned from one of his books), produces a dull if frightening roar.

His bedroom is comparatively spare, embellished only, beyond the pale gray color of the walls, by his collection of books, a large dark sculpture of Xangô and an enormous Bororo feather crown pinned to the wall at the head of his bed.

It is the contents of his desk and nightstand that I know best, that are the most compelling, most revealing about him, for mostly they are personal items, which, curiously, perversely, he felt no reason to take with him or hide: the old pocket watch and ribbon, the fancy pens and paper, and the nickel-plated pistol he keeps for protection in a drawer by his bed.

There too I found a binder of some hand-written drafts of his own mimetic verse, which I read without interest one night, just after I'd arrived, scarcely moved by the unctuous lines. Yet who am

I to judge his work, his talent, as his poetry has been published in numerous literary journals, both here and abroad, as I discovered one day while browsing the internet, most notably in France where he appears to have developed a small if avid following. The fact is not surprising, for even in Portuguese his style is plainly reminiscent of Rimbaud.

It is only now that I remember my dream from this morning, a dream about Fernão, this man I've never met but through the silent proxy of his things. I was sitting on the floor in the empty kitchen of the house across the street last night, rereading some of the letters Zweig and Lotte had written while in Buenos Aires, to where, in the fall of 1940, he'd been invited as part of a radio tour of Argentina, and thinking idly about the performance they'd seen there one night, Humperdinck's dark fairy opera, *Hansel and Gretel*, when, not even hearing the wind pick up outside, hearing only the mystic ticking of my watch, I drifted off to sleep.

In the dream, having just returned from a walk in the hills, I'd found Fernão, dressed in some sort of custodial uniform and cap, sweeping the stairs of the building; I heard the squeaking of the elevator in the shaft beside me, though I knew it wasn't working, something about a part from Japan, and I remember being surprised to find that he was already back from France, that his sister had failed to warn me of his return.

I felt sick with panic, for I'd neglected to wash the breakfast dishes that morning, had left them on the kitchen table without bothering to rinse off the yolk and jam, and was struggling to think of a way to get round him without detection, as he hadn't seen me yet, so intent was he on sweeping the stairs, when much to my horror I cried, "Eggs and beans and coffee and potatoes!" to which, not fazed, it seemed, but still sweeping, he crooned, "For now the cupboard is bare."

Somehow I'd remembered the song, the words. Years before I had seen the opera in Berlin, had not liked it, and might never have thought of it again had it not been for Lotte's reference to it in one of the letters I'd read last night.

In truth I'd scarcely remembered the performance, who was singing, what the sets were like, or even where in the vast Deutsche Oper Berlin I'd been seated that night. I'd had a bad cold, I remember that, and had drunk too much wine at dinner in the overheated restaurant of my hotel, feeling sullen and angry at a friend of mine, a woman I'd met at a conference one year, who'd suddenly cancelled our date for the evening, thereby forcing me to spend my last long evening alone.

What had saved me that night, what in that end had diverted me from myself, from my cold, from the empty seat beside me in the opera house, what had buoyed my spirits as the broom maker sang and the sounds of the orchestra swelled darkly around me, was purely the result of chance, of a conversation I'd overhead at dinner just an hour or so before.

Behind me at a table in my hotel where I'd eaten my dinner that evening, two women (one of them a poet, I'd learned) had been discussing a painting called 'Back from Market' that they'd seen together in the Louvre, and about which, long ago, the poet had written a poem, which poem, after some cajoling, she'd agreed to recite for her friend, then and there, so as to conjure the painting between them as they'd paid their bill and gathered up their things, the poet intoning softly, amidst the genial clatter of silverware and plates, "Dressed in the colors of a country day..."

And that was it. She'd shared nothing more of the poem as she'd threaded her way past me toward the door, as if suddenly self-conscious in the busy, overheated restaurant, or as if—her mind muddled by the heat, the wine—she'd merely forgotten the words, written so long ago, in some other mood or place, or perhaps she'd arrested her words so abruptly with no other aim than to tease me, their auditor, the eavesdropper, granting me but that single fine line before ducking her way out the door.

At once, once I'd returned to my room upstairs, I'd looked up the poem (as well as the painting itself, which I'd never seen before, had known nothing about) and read it aloud and in my head until I knew it by heart, so that later, when I'd recalled the opening stanzas in the darkness of the opera house that night, it had banished from the world all violence and hazard and death:

> Dressed in the colours of a country day—
> Grey-blue, blue-grey, the white of seagulls' bodies—
> Chardin's peasant woman
> Is to be found at all times in her short delay
> Of dreams, her eyes mixed
> Between love and market, empty flagons of wine
> At her feet, bread under her arm. He has fixed
> Her limbs in colour, and her heart in line.
>
> In her right hand, the hindlegs of a hare
> Peep from a cloth sack; through the door
> Another woman moves
> In painted daylight; nothing in this bare
> Closet has been lost
> Or changed. I think of what great art removes:
> Hazard and death, the future and the past,
> This woman's secret history and her loves—

Since then, since that night in Berlin, I've seen the painting twice (once in Paris, at the Louvre, and once, by chance, in Rotterdam, when it was there on loan), and each time with a kind of double vision, that is, through my own eyes overlain with the eyes of another, those of the poet herself, whose sense of the poem is now inseparable from my own.

Oddly I was not surprised to discover the next day, while rummaging around in the stereo cabinet beneath Fernão's television, and still thinking about my dream, that he is in fact familiar with the opera *Hänsel und Gretel*, that he owns a recording of it, a digitally re-mastered version of the 1953 release starring Elisabeth Schwarzkopf and Elisabeth Grümmer in the title roles.

As I'd scarcely remembered the music from that night in Berlin, I'd spent the better part of the afternoon that day listening to the opera on his stereo, sipping rum and staring out the window at the house across the street, mesmerized by the keenly paired voices, engrossed in the darkly stilted scores.

When later I'd played a few selections from it for Lurdes, to see what she thought of it, what she would say about her fat, ungrateful brother who wrote poetry, lived in Paris, and enjoyed such music as that, she'd said nothing at all to me, merely gurgled with joy, smiling, sighing, and bobbing her kerchiefed head.

She was still humming the tunes the next day when she brought me her newspaper to read with my coffee, just as she was still humming them that evening in her kitchen as she washed the dishes, clinking the plates and silverware, and banging her pots and pans.

It occurred to me then, as it occurs to me now, triggered then, somehow, by the opera Lurdes was humming, and by her banging her pots and pans, that perhaps she has not only wondered about where it is I go at night but has actually seen it for herself, many times, has watched me from her window as I crossed the street below, started down the hill toward the center of town, as though bent on some errand there, only to turn abruptly on my heels. She would have seen me making my way back up the hill past our building, with its busy ground-floor market, seen me pass the empty, overgrown house across the way and continue on up the hill, as if suddenly bound in that direction instead, just to reverse my course once more, at the bend in the road where the bougainvillea overtops the wall (she would have to have leaned out her window to see me there), swiftly retracing my steps to the very place I'd begun, just minutes before, only to stand casually, insouciantly, before the dark shuttered house on the hill, standing focused and still, as if taking aim at the house with a camera—a journalist, a tourist, some heartsick, some footsore *flâneur*, though in fact only thinking, waiting, gazing up at the star-lit sky through the towering, flowering trees until some grumbling and inevitable old man or housewife passed me by with a wary *Boa noite*, when I'd vanished like a specter through the gate.

Had she been watching me then, had she been watching me still, she would have seen me scramble my way up the steep embankment before the house, would have followed my bobbing white shirt amidst the hydrangeas on the hill and moments later seen the flicker of my flashlight inside. Or she might have seen the light by chance one night, never having wondered what it is I do at dusk, that gloaming interregnum between dogs and wolves, preoccupied with her knitting and TV, and with her worries about her son, about his epilepsy and his drinking, drawn to the window that night by chance and chance alone, by a familiar voice in the street or by some sudden bright impulse to see the sky. With her television on and her head full of worries, she might never have heard me leave my apartment at all, never heard the jingling of my keys in the lock, never seen me pacing the empty sidewalk below, as if waiting for a girlfriend, a bus. Distracted by the telephone, by her son's drunken pleading, by one of her novels, by some hero's reckless cunning, she might never have noticed my bright white shirt bobbing like a cork upon that restless sea of hydrangeas after all, so that when by chance (she is not a suspicious woman) she glimpsed the light inside the house across the street, saw it moving from room to room one night as she listened to the radio or readied herself for bed, clipping her toenails or pulling a comb through what remains of her once-fine black hair, she might never have thought of me at all, her *americano, o estudioso, o professor,* but of some common burglar who had found his way in, though the house was empty, she knew, had been empty for years, was cursed and deserted with nothing left in it to steal. She might have seen it, the light, and simply gone to bed, not thinking about me but huddled over my books next door, might hardly have given it another thought, the light, brushing her teeth and grumbling righteously about kids these days, boys with girls who spread their skinny legs, or she might have noticed the light as she finished the dishes one night, the forks and spoons, the pots and pans, glimpsed it, a comet, a flash, in the corner of her eye, as she rinsed out a teacup or saucepan or plate, and thought with a shudder of the crime rate in Rio, of a story she'd heard on the news that evening, that morning, that Sunday at church, a story meant to stir and discomfit one, a tale about the criminals in Rio who'd begun to reach their long and greedy fingers here, to Petrópolis, where the children are healthy, where the air and streets are clean, she might have seen the light flicker there between the shutters where she had never seen a light flicker before, and gasped at the not so irrational fear of them (the criminals, their fingers), crossing herself twice before calling the police.

But no, she is too smart, too curious, for that. Instead of calling the police, who would have knocked at her door, as they had knocked at her door before, pressing their way into her tiny kitchen with their crackling radios and their heavy black boots, rather than calling the police, who would have asked her about her son (his whereabouts, his friends), rather than risk such humiliation again, with no husband to defend or console her, she would have watched me from her window each night without doing or saying a thing, would have watched me with a fixed and placid expectation, never even thinking of the police or of the criminals in Rio, rapt as a child at the movies where she sat there in her kitchen window, intrigued, excited, by my nightly routine.

I imagine her thinking: *What's he want with that old house? What's he up to in there?* And I imagine her chuckling to herself at the thought of my duplicity, at my thinking myself so clever, so sly, so that each time we meet now, each time she sits with me to play a little chess or to talk about the news, about the war in Iraq, about the latest rash of murders in Maceió, that violent city by the sea where she was raised, where she studied French and fell in love, each time she looks at me, fingering a rook where she sits here in the kitchen, smoking her cigarettes and nursing her thimble of rum, each time she speaks to me about Francisco José, raising her eyes and crossing herself before the rustic saints on my wall, each time she grieves to me about her handsome and prodigal son, about his children in São Paulo, who are his and not his and whom he has never let her know (Abilio, dark Tisa, and the cocksure Clemente), each time she worries herself sick about him, her precious 'Francisquinho,' lamenting his seizures and his drinking, which have kept him from meaningful work, which have kept him from finding a proper girl, each time she speaks about anything at all these days, I find myself distracted by the weight of what she knows, which lends even her lightest, most colloquial expressions a tension and shadow and weight.

For one of these days she will speak her mind to me, she will ask me, this angel of loss, this widow of the world with her handsome, ailing son, she will ask me what it is I do in there, in that house across the way. She will ask me about Zweig, about the sort of man he was, the sort of man who could murder his pretty young wife, who could bring her here from Europe, from Hitler, to a house like that, only to kill her in her sleep. She will ask me that one day and I will have to be patient with her. I will have to grant her her say.

Then perhaps, once she has shrugged her shoulders and sighed, I will tell her the truth about Zweig, about his friends and celebrity in Europe, about the burning of his books, about his anguished flight from the Nazis, the war. And I will tell her about his first and second wives.

Only when it seems she has reckoned the words, when at last she has chewed them up and swallowed them, will I tell her about his suicide here, about his and Lotte's death in the house across the way, how, during a brief sojourn in Rio, where they'd gone with friends to see the floats and costumes of Carnival, and to enjoy a film in the newly opened theatre on Cinelândia Square, they'd suddenly returned to Petrópolis, spurred, panicked, by the news that a German submarine had just sunk a Brazilian ship in the harbor, only to discover, upon their return, that two policemen had called at the house that morning to ask them about their papers. Such signs had seemed clear to them, they were patent enough, so that they'd wasted no time in making their final preparations, returning their borrowed books, signing their farewell letters, and swallowing their pills, the barbiturates they'd set aside for themselves (she with water, he without), before embracing each other without speaking in one of the hard single beds.

I will tell her this, seasoning her heart with rum, though she will refuse to believe it, I know. She will refuse to believe in a love like that, the love of such a bright, young woman for such an effete and selfish old man. She will refuse to believe it, my version, my insistence—whatever people say—that he didn't kill her, this Elisabet Charlotte Altmann, but had loved her dearly, truly. She will deny it all, shaking her head at me and flashing her gold teeth, only to start again, to retail for me, with her peculiar conviction for untenable things, first one and then all of her many pet theories about Zweig, insisting to me, as she has insisted before, that he tricked his young wife into taking the pills (perhaps suggesting them as something for her asthma) or drugged her food when she wasn't looking (perhaps the maid herself was complicit) or (and this she will argue most vehemently, examining my features, my face) had by then so thoroughly isolated his pretty young wife from the world around them, from their friends and family in Europe and America, from even their friends and neighbors in Brazil, had by then so completely sequestered her here in Petrópolis, high in the mountains, deep in the jungle, that she could no longer depend on even the simple consolation of reading the daily news (for she barely read the language at all) but had to rely on him, her husband, for any real measure of the world, had to draw her daily sustenance, her very sense of self, from him and him alone, that vain and moribund man who'd hated the language for the way it crippled him, made a fool of his heart, his tongue, though he could read it with effort if he had to, and did, if always with a dictionary and phrasebook in hand, so hungry, so desperate was he for even a glimpse of that gracious, glittering life he'd left behind him in Vienna, the sumptuous gardens and stately avenues, the crowded concert halls and theatres, the brisk winter walks in the Wiener Wald, requiring here, with his mosquitoes, with his flea-bites and fog, but the slightest stimulus (a song, an expression, a whiff of wet woolens) to carry him back there, to the Musikverein and the Stadtpark in winter, to the noble chestnut alleys, to the beloved company of his friends and admirers in the many well-known cafes (*Café Hawelka, Café Sperl,* and his favorite, the lavish and popular *Imperial*), while knowing in his heart, his bones, that he would never return, *could* never return, that the Europe he longed for was gone, defiled, destroyed (*Io non mori,' e non rimasi vivo*), his devoted readership scattered, laid waste, knowing each and every day, as he edited his Balzac or read his Montaigne, while sucking the bitter aspirins Lotte gave him for his teeth, that he himself was already dead, ashes, dust, as dead as the table, the ashtray, as dead as the print on the page before him, knowing each and every night, when he and Lotte sat together on the wide covered terrace, adrift above the village, the palm trees, the rain, and she asked him about the news, about Vienna and Paris, about London and Salzburg and Bath, gently pressing him for an anecdote, some story to amuse her

while she darned a sock or coddled their little dog Plucky in her
freshly aproned lap, knowing each and every time she turned her
pretty young face to him and spoke of home, eager for news about
their friends and family, and about Vienna itself, for any memen-
tos, reminders (the murky scent of Saint Stephen's, the taste—her
favorite—of yeast buns and cream), knowing each and every time
she looked at him and sighed that he'd been dead for months now,
like the man from Grillparzers' play, an effigy, a sack of ashes and
gravel, though she couldn't see it, poor girl, couldn't stop him from
naming the world for her, there with the rain where they sat, the
flowers and birds, the comets and planets and stars, so that by
the end she'd had no choice but to believe him when he told her
that Hitler and his madness had triumphed, that the Nazis (*Heil
Hitler!*) would soon be marching their way through Brazil.

And again I'll say nothing to discourage her but wait until she
is done, when I will do my best to correct her. For she speaks, this
woman who knows nothing of Zweig but what she has gathered
from hearsay, from her friends and neighbors in the street, she
speaks (as your mother too once spoke, Yaniv, when she was angry
and restless and pregnant with you) as if Zweig's life were nothing
but a novel written to amuse an idle reader in the empty hours
before bed, a tale of romance, of adventure, in which the author
had felt free to embroider the truth, to manipulate the facts to
suit him, omitting this or that detail, jumbling the sequence, even
invoking mayhem and murder, if it served his lurid ends.

Still I know what she means, I know what she is after: we tell
the stories we *need* to tell, the tales that serve us best.

Zweig himself was not exempt from this propensity. A land of
the future, indeed! That's what he'd called the country, the phrase

he'd used as the subtitle of his much maligned, now little-read book about Brazil. He'd borrowed it from a letter he'd read by an Austrian diplomat named Count Prokesch-Osten, who, in hesitating to accept the embassy post here in 1868, had reasoned sternly, as if as a list to himself: "A new place, a magnificent port, distance from shabby Europe, a new political horizon, a land of the future, and an almost unknown past that invites the scholar to do research, a splendid natural setting, and contact with exotic new ideas."

It was virtually the same experience that had been recorded nearly four hundred years earlier by the Portuguese chronicler, Pero Vaz de Caminha, who had accompanied Admiral Pero Álvares Cabral, in one of his thirteen small ships, on his first voyage to Brazil. What he wrote combined keen, empirical observation with the neophyte's delight in the exotic, the strange, a wistful, ulti-mately fatal fascination with the land and its natives, with those children of nature, those dark, naked Adams who knew "nothing of bread, wine or money."

So Zweig too had thought of Brazil when he and Lotte arrived here from New York aboard the *S.S. Uruguay* in 1941. Tired, anx-ious, he'd found the land Canaan, a paradise of people and birds, a latter-day Eden, writing giddily from their sea-side terrace at the Hotel Central:

> All shades, all nuances of physiology and character
> can be found here. Anyone who crosses the street
> in Rio sees more peculiarly mixed and already
> indeterminable types in an hour than he would
> otherwise see in another city in a year. Even chess,
> with its millions of combinations, none of which

repeats itself, seems deficient in comparison with this chaos of variation, hybrids, and crosses into which inexhaustible nature has fallen during four centuries here... What characterizes the Brazilian physically and spiritually is above all the fact that he is more delicately natured than the European or North American. The large, massive, tall, large-boned type is almost entirely absent. Similarly, in the spiritual dimension—and one feels it is a blessing to see that demonstrated thousands of times over within a nation—any brutality, violence, vehemence, and loudness, everything course, boastful, and arrogant is missing. The Brazilian is a quiet person, inclined to be wistful and sentimental, sometimes even with a slight trace of melancholy... Class and racial hatred, that poisonous European plant, has not yet taken root here.

Of course he was wrong about that. Not only had that 'plant' taken root here, but it had begun to flower, bear fruit, for, while the Nazis had not in fact landed in Rio, the German Army then locked in a bitter offensive against Russian forces in Kharkov, the Brazilian president, dictator, and would-be suicide, Getúlio Vargas, who himself had welcomed the Zweigs to Brazil before the flashing cameras, toasting the famous writer at the quayside and kissing his pretty young wife, this 'populist' and reformer, this 'reluctant revolutionary,' this kindly 'Father of the Poor,' was even then hard at work on the creation of his own *Estado Novo*, banning political parties, silencing the press, jailing communists, intellectuals, and artists, and passing laws that severely restricted Jewish immigration to Brazil, what was surely the death-knell for thousands of Jews still trapped in Europe…

But again I move too quickly, too fast.

By late 1941 the Zweigs were comfortably settled in their little house here in Petrópolis. Zweig was writing well, they had made some friends in the neighborhood, and had bought themselves a dog, a wire fox terrier that slept on a pillow at the foot of their beds. Yet already the tiny crystals of doubt were hatching in his brain; already his spirit had dimmed. In a letter to friends he writes:

> …I have started already new work and life is at least here so easy. Let us describe our day; morning a delicious Brazilian coffee, then on the verandah work and reading, a primitive lunch, a game of chess, a walk and work again—we spend nearly nothing, I have not been in a theatre since a year, in a concert since half a year. I see strictly nobody for weeks, but the surroundings are mar-velous, the climate agreeable, it is a monkish life but a very healthy one and this was necessary. I must confess that I had a break down with black thoughts what all may happen (and some of it may happen/Lotte was only bones and cough for weeks; now I feel more indifferent against all possible annoyances and worries and Lotte looks much better, we live together like turtle-doves and try to forget the world… *ich hab mein Sach' auf nichts gestellt.*

I see him now, as I have seen him before, sitting on the edge of his bed in his shirtsleeves and tie. Patiently, nervously, he studies his mustache and lips in the poorly silvered mirror he keeps in the drawer by his bed. It is hot; the fan turns beside him; his face glistens with sweat. He too is waiting for the night to settle in, for the dogs to stop their barking, for the bats—those Cossacks—to commence their twilight raids. His lips are lustless, thin; his mustache needs trimming, and for a moment he wonders where his scissors are, when with a pleasant pang he recalls his barber shop in Vienna, in the tidy Josefstadt district where he'd lived—the hot towel shaves, the snip-swishing of scissors, the manly ambrosia of tonics and balms. He is vain, he knows: he likes a crease in his trousers. Some days the hairs on his pillow are enough to make him weep. Yet tonight his mind rebels: amazed, he pictures the Hindu goddess, Kali, as he saw her in Calcutta, the black skin, the pasted tongue, the gaudy bright necklace of skulls. He remembers a cremation at the river's edge, the camphor smoke, the crowds; he remembers the skull popping, the soul set free. In Hinduism there *is* no History, his friend Romain Rolland once told him. He'd said the name Kali meant *Time*.

Parting the curtain now, I check the hour, the light. Suddenly the bats have appeared in the trees above Zweig's house. I see the manager of the corner restaurant emerge through the back door of the bar to smoke a cigarette on the sidewalk, as he does around this time each night, a balding man about my age who lives with his pregnant girlfriend in an apartment a couple of streets away, where in the mornings I have seen them walking her dog by the canal. The restaurant, always popular, is particularly busy this evening; the small patio, lit festively with strings of colored lights, is already crowded with revelers. Even from here I can feel the rhythmic thumping of the music from inside and am tempted to cross the street for a quick drink and something to eat, but resist the urge, for there is still so much to think about, to do.

It is my favorite time of day, of night, the hour when a grateful hush settles over the neighborhood, the dogs stop barking, and high above Zweig's house the silhouettes of the great *ipê* and *embaúba* trees appear engraved upon the sky.

It is now, at dusk, that I often think of you, Yaniv, of your life there in Haifa. As ever I picture it raining there, a light rain falling through the leaves. I picture you in your room at night, talking on the telephone, playing a game on the computer, perhaps gazing out at the darkness as it settles over the steep ravine behind your house. Around you there are books and posters and in the corner by the door a guitar that you sometimes try to play. And some-where in the room is a picture of your mother for which you have found a simple frame or perhaps no frame at all but have pinned to the board above your desk. As surely the house is filled with photographs of her (posing in the backyard, the kitchen, hamming with you at the beach), I suspect that the photo in your room is a special one, an older one, one you discovered by chance one day in a box of your mother's things, a box your step-father had set aside for you for later, when you were grown, some white-bordered black and white snapshot of your mother when she was young and so pretty, when she was young and so pretty and overcome with her pretty young life, the lightly faded photograph taken long ago, before you were born, in a place you don't know, don't recognize, by a person you've never met, taken with some old Leica or Zeiss, perhaps taken by me, with *my* old Leica or Zeiss, though you'd never know it, would have to guess it by my shadow (if there was one) or by the look in your mother's eyes. For I know that you have chosen a photo in which your pretty young mother is looking right at you, as if she sees you where she stands before some bookshop or bodega or sits among the pigeons in Washington Square Park, as if about to kiss you, stroke your hair, as if about to whisper your name.

Sometimes when I picture you there in Israel, you are younger, maybe nine or ten, and your mother is still alive. I see you, the two of you, laughing in the yard, planting bulbs together, playing catch beneath the trees. I see you spraying your mother with a hose: she is laughing, the sunshine sparkles on the grass, and I know that you are loved, that in your lonely young life there you are never alone.

Even as I imagine you now, in that distant country, in that city by the sea, there in your room with your mother dead and your step-father making dinner downstairs, I see you happy somehow, kicking a soccer ball in the street, roaming the dusty hillside behind your house, and laughing over nothing with friends. I see you going to college, serving in the army, getting a job, and falling helplessly in love. And every day I fear for your life there, Yaniv. Every day I read the papers fearing that one day you will be blown to bits while out shopping, while eating falafel at a restaurant with friends, that one day, maybe someday soon, the whole world will come crashing down on your head without you ever knowing why. This I fear when I close my eyes at night, this I fear when I wander the streets here by day, when I lie here in this apartment, this bed, looking up at the thick, roiling clouds through the dark and trembling trees. So monstrous is the prospect to me that some days I cannot even think of you but to despair, for there are so many things I wish to tell you now that I fear I will never be able to tell you them all. This I fear and dread, that I haven't the time to explain such things, let alone to explain myself—who I am, why I left you, why in all these years I've never tracked you down, never demanded to see you, never sent you so much as a letter, a card, I do not know, I cannot say, though surely it must puzzle you, Yaniv. Even now my mind goes blank when I try to fathom your hurt, your confusion, your rage. Some days I stagger under the weight of what I've done, of what I've failed now forever to do, so that it's a wonder I'm still here at all, still breathing, still thinking of you, when twice this past winter I stood alone by the Hudson at night, staring hard at the groaning, jagged floes, and at the dark, unwholesome spaces between, through which a body, a being, might slip. On two occasions I wandered there to the edge of the river to watch the ice crack and cleave as in some prehistoric dream, knowing at last that something must give, that my life in that city was done.

I was here in Brazil, in Rio, the day the World Trade Center was attacked by terrorists for the second time. I'd spent the morning head buried in books in the Biblioteca Nacional, and had only learned of the attack later that day, when I'd returned to my hotel to find the lobby still crowded with people crying and exclaiming and jockeying for position around the large television behind the bar there, transfixed, bewitched, by the pictures on the screen. Someone cried that New York had been attacked, that the Twin Towers had collapsed, that hundreds, maybe thousands, were dead.

Sure enough it was true. That night on the television in my room I'd watched the airplanes strike the towers again and again, in the same nightmarish loop, seen the smoke and flames, seen the workers trapped high in the buildings leap out into the blue.

By the time I'd returned to New York some many weeks later I'd hardly recognized the place—the long lines at Customs, the body searches, the strutting young soldiers with their bomb dogs and guns. I'd arrived to find the military in charge, the nation the subject of de facto martial law, a change with which my compatriots had seemed delighted, seemed *pleased*, grinning coyly at the soldiers and security guards, whispering reverently, and holding hands as they made their way through the tightly cordoned maze at Customs as though charged, in their very submission, by some numinous resolve.

I myself had felt sick; it had made my blood run cold—the officiousness and solemnity, the flags and bunting, the fawning, the bigotry, the glee. I'd wanted to get away, to catch the next flight back to Rio without ever setting foot on U.S. soil, but had been swept along through the gate on the tide of softly bleating travelers.

The nation was mobilizing itself for war. Hailing a taxi, I'd seen it in the faces, I'd felt in the air, and had tried despite myself to embrace the anger and vengeance that were my birthright, my due. I'd pictured the Towers, the clear blue sky; I'd imagined the heady throng of traders, secretaries, and CEOs armed for the day's battle with their laptops and cell phones, and as in perpetual replay I'd seen the airplanes strike the towers, seen the smoke and flames, seen the towers crumble to dust. I'd thought of other times, other wars; I'd juggled the places, the motives, the names, and—yes!—I'd felt something after all, a tingling of righteousness, a twinge of some ancient and formidable rage.

Yet it was nothing I could sustain. What I'd felt above all was fear, a terrible grinding fear that great wheels had been set in motion that would take generations to bring to rest again. I'd wanted to run and hide. I'd wanted to cringe and cower until the smoke had fully cleared, for if war was courage I was a coward at heart.

Zweig too had hated war, not simply for its destruction, its carnage, but for the naked outrage of it, the abomination, the folly. For Zweig, war was a betrayal of the human spirit itself. Righteous, blind, it corrupted everything—art and memory, language and love, so that even here in Brazil, a world away from Hitler, he'd felt trapped by the language and culture that had made him.

"Heroism: Instead of an Introduction" is the title of Victor Klemperer's preface to his eccentric study, *The Language of the Third Reich (Lingua Tertii Imperii)*, his 'philologist's notebook' about the strategic Nazi conquest of the German people themselves by means of their own language, a work he'd written and compiled in secret while living in Berlin. Saved from certain death by his conversion to Christianity and by his marriage to an 'Aryan,' he'd managed— despite his disgust, his despondency, and for all his desire to cut himself off from the present, to retreat into his books, to bury his head in the sand—to record in detail, as it was happening around him, the coordinated Nazi assault on the German language.

Each day he'd read the papers, listened to the radio, and followed civilians and soldiers through the streets, recording for posterity the many changes in their day-to-day moods and expressions, the sudden, sometimes subtle shifts in their syntax and diction. He'd collected envelopes and postcards, advertisements and flyers; from the waste bins he'd retrieved boxes and bottles and cans, scouring their labels for clues. And the change he'd witnessed was chilling. In a matter of months he'd noted the way the spirit of Nazism had permeated the flesh, the blood, the very marrow of even the people he knew best, fellow professors, his neighbors, even his housekeeper, his wife, had seen the way it twisted their tongues and hardened their hearts, so that, like tiny doses of arsenic (to use Klemperer's own analogy) that at first are swallowed and digested unnoticed, yet eventually prove toxic, even fatal, the language of the Third Reich, that brash, sneering vulgate of 'Horst Wessel-Lied', had at first seemed scarcely distinguishable from the German he knew, the German of Goethe, Hölderlin, and Schiller, the German in which he dreamt and wrote and made love to his wife, only to flourish suddenly, like a cancer in his brain, muddling his instincts and clouding his very ability to reason, to *see*.

Strafexpedition (punitive expedition) was the first term he recognized as being specifically National Socialist. He wrote it down. There was *Volkstumlich* (Populist) and *historisch* (historical) and *Staatsakt* (state occasion); there was *artfremd* (alien), *Untermensch* (subhuman), *Rassegenossen* (racial comrades), and *Weltjudentum* (global Jewry); there was *spontan* (spontaneous), *kämpferisch* (aggressive, belligerent), and *fanatisches Gelöbnis* (fanatical vow). He wrote them all down. Then there was the simple *heroisch* (heroic), perhaps the most fateful perversion of all. This too he wrote down, making a note each time he read it somewhere, each time, and in what context, he heard it said.

In his book, *Mein Kampf*, Hitler had set out his general principles of education, principles devoted not to the mind but the body, to what he'd called *körperliche Ertüchtigung* or physical training. He'd believed that in education the physical must always predominate, must be privileged over the restless, seditious workings of the mind, as only the body could be properly molded, only the body could be loyal and true.

It was from this initial formulation that the concept of the Nazi hero emerged, observed Klemperer, so that soon "anything and everything heroic on land, at sea and in the air wore a military uniform." Under Hitler the battlefield was everywhere at once: "… military heroism is stored in every factory, in every cellar; children, women, and old people die one and the same heroic death…" *Der Totale Krieg* (total war), Hitler had called it, so that no matter where Zweig fled (to France and England, to the United States, finally here, to Brazil) there was no escaping it; he'd stood no chance at all. Not even in his dreams had he been able to find some peace of mind but had stalked the lonely rooms here at night, while Hitler, *Herr Hitler*, danced a jig upon his head.

Now the house across the street is dark, its outline barely visible against the overgrown hillside. Lurdes has seen it in her dreams, the house, seen it trembling in the darkness, seen it burst into flames. She trembles when she tells me this, trembles as if the floor itself is shaking, trembles like the house itself in her dreams. She can never find the words for the flames, the words for the colors, the heat, though she babbles away at me in her innumerable, incomparable tongues, attesting, avowing, until she's exhausted herself with her grim compounding and rum. For such is her faith these days, a mixture of Jesus and liquor and dread.

The sun has finally set. Rinsing my glass in the sink, I try the bathroom one more time.

Above the toilet hangs a lithograph of São Judas Tadeu, the saint of impossible losses. Why Lurdes' brother chose to hang it in the bathroom is anyone's guess. One of the twelve apostles of Jesus, Jude is usually depicted holding an image of Jesus and either a club or a carpenter's rule. Sometimes his head is ringed with fire. Yet the likeness above the toilet is different: in the faded lithograph Jude is holding a book (probably his own Epistle). Crowned by a golden nimbus with stars, he wields not a club but an axe.

Legend has it that he was born into a poor Jewish family in Palestine from where he traveled widely, preaching the Gospel in Judea, Samaria, Idumaea, Syria, Mesopotamia, and Libya. On a trip through Lebanon he was beaten to death then beheaded with an axe, so that each time I urinate I think of him—his faith, his martyrdom, his soft, subjunctive eyes.

I manage nothing but a trickle this time, though my bladder feels full. Briefly, before switching off the light, I examine my eyes, I consider my damp and sallow skin.

It is finally time, Yaniv: the dogs have stopped barking, the sky dark above Zweig's house. Into my backpack I stuff a journal, some pens and pencils, my thermos of coffee, and the slender black flashlight I bought in a shop in town. I check the pocket for extra batteries and snap it closed. All that remains is to pack up my laptop and go.

"It is quite small, really only a bungalow," writes Lotte Zweig in a letter to her mother, not long after they'd arrived here from Rio. Indeed the house is modest, even austere—four small rooms with an outbuilding where the servants once lived. Were it not for the covered terrace and its view of the valley and mountains beyond, the house would seem smaller still.

As usual I have settled myself in the bedroom, with its warped wooden floor and drab damask wallpaper, now peeling in strips by the door, the narrow little room in which Zweig and Lotte had slept and dreamt and pledged their hearts to death.

Around me I have arranged my things: my journal, my pens and pencils, and my thermos of coffee, strong dark coffee, which I've sweetened with a little cream. The only light in the room, the only light I need, is the light from my laptop screen.

All told, getting in was easy tonight: no impediments, no surprises, that is, except for the lock on Fernão's door, which stuck again, forcing me to sound a racket with my keys as I made my way out. Fortunately Lurdes' door was closed. A little hard of hearing, she was watching TV.

Hot as it is tonight, I'd not been surprised to find the sidewalk in front of my building crowded with the usual late-night shoppers, housewives mostly with broken-backed sandals and poorly dyed hair who'd eyed me with suspicion when I'd appeared in their midst.

By now they know me, by sight if not by habit, by name, for surely Lurdes has told them about me, her tenant, her American, *o estudioso*, *o professor*, has tempted them with at least a few details about my curious presence here, as she sniffed the papayas or tallied up her coupons for milk and shampoo.

They are not unfriendly, the women, only wary, culturally, perhaps genetically, predisposed to question the motives of men like me. Surely they are the ones responsible for filling Lurdes' head with all her nonsense about Zweig, having learned of him themselves from their mothers, from their grandmothers and aunts, who perhaps had served him in a shop one morning, had known his cook or gardener, or had passed him in the street one day and drawn their own conclusions, hard, unsprung women whose daughters, granddaughters, and nieces now gather beneath my window each night with their broken-backed sandals and poorly dyed hair, chatting and laughing, and surveying the brightly lit sidewalk for strangers, *estrangeiros*, like me.

Tonight I'd passed them with a kindly *Boa noite*, feeling for my wallet as a reflex, only to repeat the gesture (For the women? For Lurdes at her window upstairs?), actually removing the billfold from my pocket and counting out the bills, the *reais*, with the comic ostentation of a mime, perhaps hoping in that way to dress my appearance on the street in an air of routine, as if I'd only ventured out, after a long stint of working, to stretch my legs or to buy some cigarettes.

In fact I'd been craving a smoke, and had started into the market downstairs, when, put off by the knot of idle shoppers by the door, and by the garish light inside, I'd changed my mind, hurrying off down the hill past the corner restaurant to the little newsstand by the pharmacy and laundromat where I like to look at the papers and to buy my cigarettes, my Rothmans and Hollywood Souza Cruz.

The owner, a balding Lebanese with large, hairy hands, had been watching a program on the television behind the counter, some game show or other, as he completed the daily crossword puzzle in one of the papers with his fat little pencil, and had handed me my cigarettes (Rothmans this time) without so much as a nod, appraising me from beneath his bushy black brows only when I'd requested a lottery ticket as well.

As usual I'd taken my time choosing the numbers, shaking my head, clicking my tongue, and looking about me for signals, for signs, a habit—half-mystical, half-blind—that never fails to disgust the bilious owner who'd snorted at me, once I'd finally made my selection, only to mock me with his usual "Good night and good luck!"

Only here in Brazil do I play the lottery, only here do I entertain such lumpen and generally ludicrous dreams as fill my head these days with the lightness of gas. Were I to win, I would give to the poor, surely, and I would set up an account for you, Yaniv— for college, a house, perhaps a brand new car, who knows? And I would give some of the money to Lurdes, enough for her to buy her apartment outright, and for her to travel to Macau, which she has long dreamt of seeing with her son.

It was just as I was leaving the newsstand, having stopped to look at the papers on the rack by the door, that the game show on the television had been interrupted by a news bulletin regarding the mysterious rash of arson attacks in the nearby city of Volta Redonda. Last night—so the plump young reporter had explained to the camera—a maintenance building in the Barra Manza zoo had been burned to the ground, the sixth such incident in less than three weeks. While no animals were injured by the fire, the zoo was scheduled to be closed until further notice. When pressed by her colleague back at the station about possible suspects and motives, the young reporter had remarked that, while the police had no good leads yet, one zoo worker had been happy to speculate that the blaze had been set by animal rights activists, fanatics the lot, while a local resident, a grizzled old man stopped in his pajamas while out walking his dog, had thought it more likely that the culprit was another disgruntled municipal employee.

But for two women chatting at the entrance to the market beneath my building, the street was empty when I'd turned the corner back onto Rua Gonçalves Dias, so that the instant I'd passed the restaurant, I'd ducked through the dusty bushes and scrambled my way up the steep embankment below Zweig's house, picking my way in the darkness along the narrow corridor between the back of the restaurant and the temporary fencing to the makeshift gate near the top.

Oddly the gate had been left ajar; a pair of shovels lay crossed upon the ground where the workmen had been digging this morning, perhaps searching for a cable or pipe. At once I'd checked the gas can I'd hidden in the bushes up the hill and was pleased to find that it had not been disturbed.

From there, from a crouch between a pair of clacking palms, I'd been able to see into Lurdes' windows across the street, with their simple lace curtains, and had been surprised to discover that both her kitchen and bedroom were empty, though the walls pulsed with the warm blue light of her television.

I was disappointed to think that she was not in fact spying on me, no conspirator after all. But then I'd spotted her—yes! Just as I was turning away I'd seen the curtain in the kitchen move, seen the flash of her glasses inside.

Making my way round to the back of the house, I'd found my usual window snugly fastened, though I'd left it unlocked this morning. I'd tried the living room windows, then those of the bedroom and bathroom, all of which had been securely latched. On a whim, on my way round to the other side of the house, where I've nearly always found a way in, I'd tried the kitchen door, which I rarely do, jiggling the knob, only to find that the door was not only not locked but had been taken completely off its hinges, just propped there in place, so that all I'd had to do was set it aside and walk in.

Now the kitchen is cluttered with tools, old sandwich wrappers, and a variety of empty soda cans; the air reeks of cigarettes and sweat. One of the walls, the wall between the kitchen and the living room (upon which I've always imagined some dark allegorical painting) has been marked with a large red X, presumably as an indication that it is to be removed as part of the remodeling, perhaps cut for a borrowed light or door.

Despite the delay, there is more evidence of the work here underway: in one corner of Zweig's bedroom, near where the small sink used to be, they've cut a hole at the base of the wall out of which they've pulled a rat's nest, a Medusa's head, of ugly black wires. It is clear that the wiring is old, no doubt as old as the house itself. In places the mice have nibbled away at the cotton casings, exposing the copper strands beneath, the rough-cut ends of which I cannot resist touching now, despite the risk, convinced as I am that they are the very wires that had carried the meager current through these walls when the Zweigs lived here, bereft and in exile more than fifty years ago, the same wires that had lit the lamp on Zweig's desk, the trusty, selfsame wires that had powered the large Philco radio that had stood like a fetish by their beds. Surely these floorboards are the same, with their scuffmarks and cracks, as are the windowpanes, the wainscoting, the door. Even the vanity in the bathroom is the same, though now the tub and toilet are gone.

Tonight I am not alone, for the moths too have found their way into the house, fluttering restlessly before my screen and brushing my face and hair with their wings. I wonder what it is they hear, what ancient, pristine sounds. For why else would they venture inside here, where they are bound to be trapped and die?

Straining my ears, I hear nothing but the faint whirring of my laptop and the scrape and scratching of palm fronds outside. Perhaps tonight it will rain.

As usual I check the war reports in *The Guardian*, *Le Monde*, and *Haaretz*. Not satisfied, I skim *El País*, *Die Zeit*, *Expresso*, and the local *O Globo*. Since the U.S. first invaded Iraq I no longer trust *The New York Times*.

The reports tonight are predictably grim: *After a brief lull in the violence, at least 50 people were killed yesterday in a car bomb attack on a police recruitment center south of Baghdad. In a recent statement the CIA admitted that there was no imminent threat from weapons of mass destruction before the 2003 invasion of Iraq. Last night former secretary of state, George P. Schultz delivered an address at the Library of Congress called 'A Changed World' in which he defended the invasion of Iraq, insisting, to great applause, "There has never been a clearer case of a rogue state using its privileges of statehood to advance its dictator's interests in ways that defy and endanger the international state system. The question of Iraq's presumed stockpile of weapons will be answered, but that answer, however it comes out, will not affect the full, justifiable and necessary action that the coalition has undertaken to bring an end to Saddam Hussein's rule over Iraq." The murder of Sunnis by Shi'ite death squads continues unabated as a nationwide response to the growing Sunni insurgency, a campaign of terror that includes kidnapping and extreme torture, such as the drilling of holes in skulls and feet. Experts now fear a full-blown civil war.*

Is there a logic to history? The question haunts me now where I sit here in the darkness in this empty house in this remote Brazilian town, with its mist-shrouded mountains like 'the hulls of capsized ships'. Can you find it on the map on your wall there, Yaniv, or on the globe that you spin when you're bored? Find Petrópolis, there near Rio, then spin it again.

I woke this morning thinking about Lurdes and chess, and about the Russian, Alexander Alekhine, who in 1927 defeated the great Capablanca in a championship match in Buenos Aires, then the longest in the history of the game. Zweig had liked them both, had admired their different temperaments, their different gambits and styles, though he, like Spielmann, had thought Alekhine would be lucky if he won a single game from the master. Yet win them he had, eventually forcing Capablanca to resign after thirty-four bouts.

Zweig had followed the match closely from Vienna, as it was recorded in the daily papers, discussing it with his friends over coffee each day, and marveling particularly at Alekhine's endgame, there in crowded *Club Argentino de Ajedrez*, at his relentless final moves:

77. R—K 5	R—R 8
78 K X P	R—K Kt 8 B
79. R—Kt 5	R—K K R 8
80. R—K B 5	K—Kt 3
81. R X P	K—B 3
82. R—K 7	Resigns.

Alekhine was reigning world champion when Zweig wrote his last novel, *Chess Story*, while in exile here, posting the finished manuscript to his editor just days before his suicide. Ostensibly about chess, the short novel was his first hard look at the Nazis and the world that they had wrought. Yet if Zweig had thought the state of things was dire then, in the summer of '42, he'd had only to have lived another year to have repented his grief. For just a month earlier, at a top-secret conference in Berlin, the senior Nazi leadership, frustrated by the stubbornly low kill-rate of Gypsies, cripples, and Jews, had formulated a plan under the direction of SS General Reinhard Heydrich for a 'total solution of the Jewish ques-tion,' known in German as *Endlösung der Judenfrage*, a scheme, a blueprint, for the immediate deportation and total extermination of the Jews. Of that Zweig had had no inkling when for the last time he'd embraced his wife here in bed. He'd known nothing of their plans, of their fleet of roving, custom-made vans (the Diamond, the Opel Blitz, the Saurer). He'd had no idea that they were already testing the efficiency of killing 'degenerates' using carbon monoxide gas.

I first conceived of the plan to return here, to Petrópolis, one damp winter day, not long after my illness was discovered. Instead of writing, I'd spent the afternoon watching the rain silver the trees along my street in Greenwich Village and reading a book about the Nazi commander, Adolf Eichmann, which I'd bought on sale one day at the Strand, a brisk, often stirring account of his capture by Mossad agents in Buenos Aires in 1960, where he, like so many high-ranking Nazis, had gone into hiding after the war.

There, outside his remote cinderblock house on Garibaldi Street, the Israeli agents had secretly abducted him one night when he'd stepped off the bus from work, then smuggled him back to Jerusalem, where he'd been made to stand trial, found guilty of crimes against the Jewish people, then hanged. Eager that he not be buried, that he not be martyred in the years to come, his remains ennobled, enshrined, the authorities had seen to it that his body was cremated at once, within hours of his execution, the ashes heaped in a bucket, covered with a damp cloth, then dumped in the sea that same night.

I'd often thought about the story in the days and weeks that followed, when I'd struggled to make sense of even the simplest things, scarcely stirring from my apartment, hardly reading, hardly thinking at all, only sitting and staring out the window at the dirty patch of sky above the trees, when suddenly I would think of

Eichmann again, of the bucket, the ashes, the small boat rocking on the waves at night, and of the men themselves—agents surely—hunched together in the dimly lit cabin somewhere far and forever at sea.

Sometimes I'd thought of them, of the boat, of Eichmann, of the bucket of ashes, while resting or reading or heating a can of soup on the stove. Sometimes they'd flashed into my mind, the images, the details, while I was standing in line at the grocery store or waiting for the subway: the bucket, the ashes, the lonely, vacant street on which Eichmann had lived, lived modestly, anonymously, as a husband and father, as an Argentine national, as a taciturn factory worker named Ricardo Klement. For weeks I'd nursed it like a secret, the strange, inchoate tale just tapping away in my head. Yet it wasn't until I'd returned here, to Petrópolis, that it all had all come clear to me, that I'd grasped what I must do.

I'd been happy to leave New York, relieved to think that I would never return. For years I'd loved the city, had wandered its dark, congested streets, had felt a part of something lonely, something brave, unwieldy, and true. I'd spent untold hours in the museums and bookshops, in the galleries, theatres, and cafes, loving it all as one loves an old uncle who spoils one with candy while roughly fondling one's crotch. For in truth I'd come to hate the city, the people, even then, had grown bored with the restaurants, the papers, the noise. For years I'd detested it all, but had forbidden myself to admit it, struggling daily, as New Yorkers must do, to protect and compound the illusion that I was blessed to be living there, at the center of the world, the crown and envy of all.

Just an hour in the Metropolitan Museum was enough to make me sick for days, the heat, the crowds, the blinding, vile surfeit of art. Not a dozen Dürer prints and paintings but one thousand and ninety-seven, not a couple of cuneiform tablets from Babylonia but two hundred and seventy-five, not a few framed leaves from Firdausi's *Shahnama* but one hundred and ninety-three. Such is the scorn, the vengeance, the greed. Not a sampling of nativities but one thousand five hundred and fifty, not a selection of Japanese prints but five thousand four hundred and forty-six, not a pair of friezes from the ancient Temple of Dendur but the Temple of Dendur itself!

All summer long I'd chafed at the crowds, the indiscriminate hordes of tourists and day-workers from the outer boroughs, and from Long Island and New Jersey, pouring out of their garish buses double-parked along the streets and avenues and gushing up the subway steps with their cell phones and shopping bags like so much vomit or blood. I couldn't bear it any more, couldn't stand the sight of it, the faces, the traffic, *the sprawling human mess*, had had to stop up my ears at the racket, the clamor, so that for days at a stretch I'd hardly emerged from my apartment but to buy more coffee and cigarettes. If there was a city outside my window, I'd scarcely known it, ignoring it, denying it, erasing it block by block in my head while I slept, so that some mornings when I'd opened the little window in my shower I'd heard nothing but seagulls, smelled nothing but marsh grass and rain.

At once I'd stopped calling my friends, ceased replying to their letters and e-mail, and had canceled my subscriptions, one and all. In a fit of pique one day, I'd emptied out my closets and drawers, stuffing the clothes (the pants and jackets, the neckties, sweaters, and shirts—but the vulgar livery of some shameless urban clown) into large plastic bags, which I'd lugged to the street. I'd done the same with my silverware and plates, not caring what became of them, disposing of much of my furniture as well, the television and stereo, the chairs and futon, the end tables, ottomans, and lamps, as well as the antique fruitwood dining set, given me by my grandmother, even the matching Hitchcock chairs that my father himself had re-caned—all of it I'd hauled to the street in the wind and rain, at all hours of the day and night, so that at first my neighbors had thought I was moving only to realize with a gasp I'd gone mad.

Yet it was my books, getting rid of them, that had given me the greatest pleasure, a giddy, breathless satisfaction, so that I'd cried with delight as I'd torn them from the shelves—the novels and poetry, the biographies and histories and plays, sometimes hurling them into the alley with a howl, sometimes dragging them by the bagful to the street, where occasionally someone had stopped to rummage through them, examining the damp, discolored volumes, the faded spines and covers, that dirty babel of tongues, glancing furtively at my windows, only to snatch a book or two before scuttling off down the street.

One day, some many weeks later, I'd found one of my books on the empty subway seat beside me, one of the same books I'd dumped in the street. I was returning from Brooklyn after a morning spent walking and talking with a friend of mine by the ruined waterfront there, a psychiatrist and recent divorcé who'd taken to prescribing himself pills. I'd recognized the book at once, Steiner's *Heidegger*, an introduction and primer, a trial and verdict really, which I'd bought while in college and read with some confusion while sitting in Washington Square Park, so that I'd spent the remainder of the subway ride to Manhattan leafing through the wrinkled, well-thumbed pages, amazed by the coincidence and intrigued by the stranger's many marks and annotations.

I remember that he or she had scribbled on the flyleaf of the book, had included in pencil (amidst a slew of cryptic notes, '*Gegenwart*,' 'sufferance,' 're-statability,' '*das Sein ist sein*,' just beneath where, years before, and with such pretensions, I'd signed and dated the page) a short grocery list (toothpaste, apples, steel wool), a surprise, a twist I hadn't expected, one for which (God knows) I hadn't been prepared, still sick with myself and now concerned about my friend. "A grocery list in a book about Heidegger!" I'd cried aloud that day and stumbled headlong from the train.

I'd taken the book, this book I'd discarded then found, this book I have here right now in my pack, I'd taken it back to my apartment that day, eager for symbols, for signs, willing it to auger, to speak, while thinking (like pulses, like sparks) of Eichmann and his ashes, of Jerusalem and Heidegger, of Heidegger, Celan, and Brazil. More than ever it had puzzled and bewitched me, this book, this book I'd abandoned then found, so that over the next few days I'd forced my way back through its pages, knowing little or nothing about Heidegger, about his Todtnauberg, his 'Black Notebooks', his 'historical-Western purpose', about his *Rede, Gerede, Dasein*, about his *being-toward-death*, about his 'Death is a way to be...' I'd swallowed it all, then spat it out, trembling, retching, until I'd shaken myself free of it, of his grim, clotted codes, so that by the time I'd left New York, my apartment, my students, my friends, by the time I'd stepped out into the dark and drafty hallway and set down my bag, set it down so that I could lock the door behind me, so that I could lock it forever, for good, by the time I'd made my way down to the street, hailed a taxi, and settled myself inside it, behind the turbaned driver, by then, by that time, New York as a city had vanished, all of it, every I-beam and tie-clip was gone.

I'd thought, before leaving, before returning here to Brazil, of renting a car and driving upstate to examine what was left of my old house, eager in a way I had never been eager to sift through remains. Again I'd poured over the photographs my uncle had sent me—the empty front hall, the boarded up fireplaces, the handsome old staircase with its broken bannister and narrow flat-turn landing. And I'd pictured the house gone, demolished; I'd pictured the splintered timbers and broken bricks, had seen myself, as in some sentimental movie, searching listlessly through the rubble, poking here and there, admiring a scrap of old wallpaper, perhaps dusting off an old teacup or shoe. For I'd watched too many films to have seen the ruins clearly, as something particular, peculiar, to me.

It was inconceivable to me that my house was not still there, where it had always been, the house in which I'd grown and suffered and played, in which at night I'd listened—at least a thousand times I'd listened—to the rackety old freight trains across the river, hooting their way through the wide, dark valley, bound for places I would never ever know, that house with its cramped attic room in which for years I'd slept beside my brother, in which for years I'd listened to the rain on the roof and to the wind in the trees, huddled deep in the comfort of my bed, that house-once-hotel with its wide planked floors, its large, drafty fireplaces, its musty old cellar of timbers and stone, that house which I'd been happy to flee, and of which I'd scarcely thought, once my parents were dead, indeed had nearly forgotten altogether by the time I'd received my uncle's note, that house-now-destroyed had caught me unawares, so that, once alone in my apartment that evening I'd found myself too restless, too anxious, to sleep. Like a vine just severed at its root, like a stream just dammed at its spring, I'd suffered that night, as the snow tumbled down outside, an emptiness, a sense of nullity, a dark and griefless grief, as if suddenly I myself—my head, my torso, my arms, my legs—was but a large phantom limb that tingled vaguely with feeling yet was no longer there.

Even then I'd known that had I made the long drive upstate I would not have seen the house itself, *the house proper*. I'd understood that had I gone to see the remains of the old house before returning here, I would not have seen even the ruins of the house I'd known and loved, that house was gone, even the ruins were gone, the house, the ruins, the ruins, the house. I would have seen the remains of the house as but emblems, mere signatures of things, I would have seen them obscurely, obliquely, I would have seen them *obscenely*, as for years I'd been cursed to see *this* house, Zweig's house, the house in which I sit right now, this house, this room, in which Zweig and his wife once lived and died, swallowing their pills, closing their eyes, and clinging together in their narrow bed here with the raw and dread-less ardor of the morally, spiritually dead.

Now I blink my eyes and consider the room about me, determined to see it truly, with all its spirits intact. I start, as I often start, by trying to picture it through Zweig's own eyes, blinking, squinting, then slowly relaxing my focus until the room swims up around me, glimmering and shimmering with *things*. I see a dead spider, a box of nails, a paint rag by the door. I consider the crystal doorknob, the empty keyhole. Tonight the wallpaper seems strangely, significantly patterned, as do the knots in the floorboards, as do the flecks of old paint on the sill. The caulking around the window is cracked and dry, so that a few of the panes are loose.

I try now, as I have tried so many nights before, to imagine the room as it was on the night of their suicide, after they'd returned from their trip to Rio, where they'd gone with friends to see the floats and costumes of Carnival. I try to recoup, to recover, that long-lost evening—the hours, the minutes, the many piddling little gestures with no place of their own in time—once they'd returned and made their decision, when they'd taken their beloved dog to the neighbor's house (I imagine Lotte telling the old woman that they'd be travelling for a few more days, saying something vague and apologetic, with more fuss than she'd intended, something about a talk, a lecture, in Manaus, though the old woman didn't hear so well, hadn't really heard her at all, grinning daftly, and holding up the restless little dog for dear Lotte to kiss), try to conjure the very mood of the house once their precious dog Plucky was gone, once the maid and gardener had been excused for the day, *until tomorrow then*, try to picture this little room as it was after Zweig had gathered the last of his papers and burned them in the yard, the postcards and letters and receipts, the black quarto ringbooks into which each day he'd copied his latest work, after they (Lotte in the kitchen, Zweig here in their bedroom) had spent the afternoon in silence, apart, sorting and packing their things, taking an inventory of who and how they'd been, of all (what little) they still might do, might say. I try with all my might to recreate the moment when finally they had crossed that threshold, the point of no return, when suddenly they'd realized that they were alone with themselves at last, that no friends would come calling, no cards or letters arrive, when finally it was evening and the street outside was quiet and they'd scarcely eaten, scarcely spoken a word, not for fear alone but for other reasons, too, doing their best to keep busy, opening and closing drawers, making notes, as if planning a vacation, a trip, all the while humming blithely to themselves, the radio on, the radio in the bedroom here tuned to one of their favorite stations, now tuned to a song they both knew: *Address unknown/Not even a trace of you/Oh, what I'd give/To see the face of you*, that quivering breach in time when they'd still had their letters to write (Lotte had arranged the paper and envelopes on the desk beside his special paperweight, a bright blue *rhetus* in glass, had sharpened their pencils, had even selected the stamps: *PALAVRA DE ORDEM DO BRASIL, AJUDE A FAZER O CENSO*). I try to imagine it, that darkly pulsing interval, when what was done was done, decided, though they'd each had more questions, silly, niggling little questions about protocol, conventions, about the proper sequence of things, as if in fact (though each of them doubted it) there was a custom for everything—even that. *And here the soul slips in.*

I feel his breathing, his pulse, and try with all my might now to picture the little room through Zweig's own eyes where he sits here on the edge of his bed, scratching his flea bites, his cheek, alert, exhausted by the petty housekeeping of death, the anxious touching and dusting and putting-away, dazed and amazed by the sudden absence of worry, the forgetfulness, the relief, feeling strangely elated with himself, and small enough at last(!), so small he might slip through the keyhole of their door instead of dying, a thought that amuses him where he sits here in his shirtsleeves and tie, though he pursues it no further, grasping one slender wrist with the calipered fingers of his other hand, only to reverse the wonted gesture, smiling vaguely, abstractly, wondering briefly about key-holes and keys, about doors ajar at night, about the sudden crash of silverware (the forks and spoons and knives) where his Lotte in the kitchen (He swears he'll remember this!) where his Lotte in the kitchen weeps a world beside a fallen kitchen drawer.

The things he must remember! The clatter, the crash. He prom-ises himself to remember it, has sworn it, a vow, refuses to forget, though already the sound is fading in his ears, the crash and clatter, the keyhole, the tears, already his mind is taken up with other things: the late-night tram descending the hill from Rhenânia, the knot in the floorboard, the wart on his hand that he has trimmed and trifled with for so long that, even now, with so much suffered, with so much decided, with so much said and done, it makes him cringe with despair. Even now it kindles his vanity, that stubborn little flame, makes him peevish, spiteful, angry, makes him want to burn it off with acid, to gouge it out with a knife, why not? Anything to be rid of it at last!

Then his thoughts turn morbid, obscene. He pictures himself dead, lungs still, heart stopped, brain static, pictures himself lying here in bed, head cocked, mouth agape, the wart on his hand still growing, though he is by every measure dead, the stubborn cells reproducing themselves, still growing despite him, so that sud-denly he wants to scream, to howl, to rend the world to pieces, so cruel, so hideous is the notion that even after he is dead and bur-ied, even after they (Stern and Feder, Rabbi Lemle, Mrs. Banfield, perhaps their friend, the poet and consul Mistral) even after they have fastened the lid on his coffin and said their final prayers, his wart—of all things!—would still grow.

He shudders, then moans, rocks gently on the balls of his feet, as if about to rise from the bed, as if about to join his wife and console her, to kneel down beside her on the kitchen floor and gather up the forks and spoons and knives, but it is too late for that, he knows, too late for such valiant little rescues as his, too late for the sun and moon, too late for the listless, uncouth stars.

Sitting here beside him I try to imagine what *too late* even means—to him, to me, what it feels like, its texture, its *time*. And is it really time at all or just its absence he feels, sitting here on the edge of his bed in his shirtsleeves and tie? I marvel: Is the absence, such absence, enough?

Of course the answer is yes: it is plenty, sufficient, *enough*, so that he looks about the room now, sadly, yes, but complacently too, for he has always liked the little room, the way the light falls in summer, the gentle patter of rain on the rooftop when he is reading or dozing, far from Europe, deep in this jungle, in bed. He likes that feeling most of all, the rain on the rooftop, the rain in the trees, yet he dreads it, too, the jungle, the monkeys, the thoughts of never seeing home, though even dread and misgiving grow old, he knows, even dread and misgiving lose their bearings, their way, misbuttoning their trousers and shirts, misplacing their glasses, their teeth, so that it is a bother to read and chew. Even dread and longing forget, misremember things, confuse the places, the sequence, the names, only to recall them, if in fragments, in shards, if in splinters, in bits, so that now it seems that even his despair has betrayed him, just when he needs it most, has recanted its vow, relinquished its part, for suddenly he remembers—yes! He remembers his beloved nanny, Margarete, her broad peasant face, her sour breath, like cream gone bad, though the breath, the taste, is his own, the face now that of their cook, Marie, who was kicked to death by a horse, when like an epiphany (he feels it first in his gums, his teeth) he recalls with a shudder the angry clatter of his father's many looms, a sound—though he'd been forbidden to enter the mills—that had sickened him, made him anxious and dizzy with glee. Now even his anguish has shortchanged him, tripped him up, left him to fend for himself, to remember, to *feel!*

Bereft, bewildered, he counts the wrinkles on his thumb, sniffs it, the still-sulfurous skin, then gingerly winds his watch, which is not the watch his father gave him, the watch his mother kept for him in her jewelry box so that he wouldn't lose it, so that he wouldn't break it while horsing around with his friends after school. It is not that watch he is wearing now but a finer, more expensive one, one he'd bought for himself while in London one day, one cold and rainy day, when, seeking cover from the rain, having forgotten his umbrella and long since lost his father's watch, he'd stumbled into a little shop near the Thames and seen it glowing in the window, the lavish grail: a whim, a crank, an extravagance really, this doctor's watch with its Scottish gold dials—one for the time, the trains, one (the little one) for heartbeats and pulses, for soft-boiled eggs.

Unfastening it from his wrist now, he considers the trusty piece, as he might the heels of his shoes at night, sniffs the worn leather band, some reptile, the stippled hide not unpleasantly sour, inspects the tarnished case, the lightly silvered dials, the retailer: Grant McCullock, the company signature: *B.W.C.*. He thinks of the lengthened Swiss movement inside, of the hairsprings, clutch wheels, and escapement, the thought of which excites in him a foggy admiration for the moribund, taciturn Swiss, whom he has never liked nor loved but admired for their simpler, nimbler parts, for their precision clockworks, for their grave good manners and faith: *I hope you've enjoyed your stay here in Switzerland*—a line, his own, that suddenly fills him with horror, with grief, when he thinks of the war in Europe, of the high broken windows, of Jews at prayer with their bashed-in skulls and teeth.

Yet what choice had he had? Gone too are Canetti, Mann, and Broch, in Paris the dead drunk Roth. To slip while boarding a train—poor Verhaeren, dear Emile! Poor Benjamin, too, poor lonely, poor shadowless Toller—what was it your shadow said? And what about Romain, his friend and idol, Romain Rolland? Is he alive or dead, he wonders gravely, for he cannot say, does not remember, but thinks in a muddle of Vivekananda and Tagore, of tidy Villeneuve, of the gloomy stone house in Vézelay where they'd often sat silent with swimming sense by a bramble of English rose.

Now how did that poem go? "In a worldless timeless lightless great emptiness Four-faced Brahma broods…" He remembers the wine and walking, the cigars, and he remembers the abbey there, sacked by Huguenots and Norman raiders, sacked (he thinks) by Moors—the tympanum and lintel with its pig snouts and pygmies, the sculpted capitals, the extended narthax from 1132. *Four-faced Brahma broods…*

And he remembers the letter, Romain's last from Vézelay, tries to recall where he put it, which cabinet, which drawer, if indeed he ever replied to it, though he is certain he did, or nearly so, he must have, for he remembers it vaguely, the letter, his reply, remembers having told him about Lotte, about her health and her Esperanto, which study had long been of interest to him. He recalls mentioning to his friend the notes they'd found pinned to their gate. Yes!

He remembers that, that he'd told him about the notes, the threats, and he remembers (he thinks he remembers) having told him of the death of their mutual friend, Count Huyn, when he recalls the letter in fact, sees the monogrammed paper, the stamp, remembers having posted it himself (the clerk, the filthy stamp gum and brush). In a flash he remembers it all, recalls having described to Romain the abundance of fruit and chocolate here (How he'd wished he could send him some!), remembers telling him at length about his walks in the mountains here with Lotte (the birds and flowers), and about his walks in the mountains alone.

He remembers it plainly now, when just as suddenly he isn't sure, shakes his head, knits his brow and frowns. He is suddenly not certain that the count is dead, Romain still living, fears now that he has only dreamt it, the Count's death, that it is in fact Romain who is dead, the Count happy and laughing somewhere. If only he could find the letter, he would know, opening drawer after drawer and dumping the contents onto the bed in a frenzy that threatens to unravel him at last, to break the night's clean spell, to arouse again in his parched, now-febrile brain that long sordid pageant of history, *a parade of all races, all passions, the tumult of empires, the war of appetites and hates, the reciprocal destruction of creatures and things—the greed that devours, the wrath that inflames, the envy that drools, and the hoe and the pen, damp with sweat and ambition, hunger, vanity, melancholy, wealth, and love*—all of it shaking him like a rattle where he stands helpless by the bed here in his shirtsleeves and tie, when he is startled by the patter of the rain at the window and looks up, his face slack and vapid with grief, looks out at the pearling drops on the wide, waxy leaves, an image, a sensation, that reminds him of nothing, of nothing but itself, of nothing but the rain and Romain...

It was a relationship, that between Zweig and the writer-mystic, Romain Rolland, that had long-vexed my colleague and rival, Phelps, who, like a man with a pebble in his shoe, had liked to tease out the noisome matter with me as we walked and talked on the numerous occasions when we'd met here in Petrópolis, and more often in Rio, where we'd frequently encountered one another in the archives of the Biblioteca Nacional, as over the years we were bound if not certain to do, as well as over breakfast at the modest Biarritz, where he'd first induced me to stay, just a couple of blocks from the beach, knowing I was usually broke and cared little for fancy things, let alone for the beach, which I've always avoided, repulsed by the crowds and by the thought of the sand on my skin.

Phelps had often pressed me over breakfast, in his leery, circumspect way, as to what I felt about Zweig and Rolland, curious to know if I thought there was ever anything *special* between them, if, in the course of my research, my investigations, I'd discovered anything telling, suggestive, about their relationship, some inscription or letter, some affectionate, some *conspiratorial* phrase, anything at all that might spur him in his work, his thinking, though he'd had little patience for my hunches and conjecture, which I'd been happy to share with him at length, cutting me short with a wave of his hand and snapping open his newspaper the instant I ceased to be useful to him, suspecting surely (if not quite willing to believe it, that I was as cagey and selfish as he) that, had I in fact discovered something special about Zweig's relationship with Rolland, that champion of Beethoven and Gandhi, whom he'd loved and admired, whose approval he'd courted for years, something revealing, significant, something sordid, unseemly, *untoward*, a key, some illustrative trait by which to reckon the man anew, I would never have shared it with him, my adversary, my rival, this he feared, he suspected, he knew, but would have kept it to myself, a gem, a pearl in a tiny velvet case, grinning inwardly, even fondling the little box beneath the table as he spoke. It is true, I confess, I would not have told him a thing, though it hardly matters now, now that he has published his book, now that he has run the race and won, though I like to console myself, even now, especially now, with the thought that, even at the end, when his contract was signed and his book was being printed, when the presses were whirring day and night, the critics nodding, the bookshops making ready for him, the orders flooding in, I like to flatter myself, here and now, even now, with the idea that even then, before his book had appeared, when he was already the talk of the town, wearing himself out with new suits and new shoes, sitting this way and that, teasing his little red beard, and strolling pensively, as a poet in a garden, perhaps chuckling wryly to himself when at home in his apartment alone, I like to think that even then he had not quite rid himself of me, of the suspicion that there was something he'd missed about Zweig, some stone left unturned, something fresh and *essential* I'd found (in the archives here in Rio, between the pages of a book, in a trussed up shoebox beneath some daft old pensioner's bed), some bauble, some keepsake, I'd discovered and withheld from him, secured like an acorn for myself, a germ, a seed from which one day something greater, fuller, from which someday something truly novel might grow. This thought alone has sustained me—until now. Until now, I say, as I no longer begrudge him his success, now that it is over and done with, now that the race to the finish is through, but feel for him, my *former* rival, a certain tangled affection, a fondness, an affinity even, that—were things not as they are—I might very well miss.

He'd liked to walk a step or two ahead of me when, together, we wandered the streets of Petrópolis here in our curious search for Zweig, turning now and then to look at me, his colleague, his rival, to appraise my expression, to consider my response to something witty, something trenchant, he'd said, while jostling me lightly with his elbow if I threatened to overtake him or merely changed up my pace.

He'd liked to lead me, to set the tempo, striding then strolling then stopping dead in his tracks to adjust his camera or backpack or shoes, all the while speaking volubly about cameras and backpacks and shoes, about Vienna and Salzburg, about his own impossibly good health (he often stopped to have me feel his pulse), and rarely missed the opportunity to mention his brief if 'importunate' friendship with the late artist Lucian Freud, a lecherous, funny, deeply sullen old man whose technique and paintings he deplored.

Phelps had no interest in me, or only a mercenary one, finding roundabout ways to grill me on whatever I was reading at the time, on wherever I had travelled most recently, on whatever (if anything special) I knew, while never (or rarely) asking anything about me, anything *personal*, that is, except as a means to an end, abruptly changing the subject the instant I strayed from the topic at hand, from whatever matter he himself had introduced for the moment, the outing, the day, say, by telling him a joke or describing a dream I'd had or by praising the guava and white cheese I'd had for my breakfast that day. He'd have none of it, no, but would turn red in the face, snorting derisively at me, as at a fractious schoolboy, before burying me in words, so that soon I gave up even trying to speak with him as cohorts, as friends, listening now and then (he could often be quite funny), and generally amusing myself as we walked by nodding my head and grunting softly like a pig, treating his voice as I would the drone of bees outside my window or the snarl of chainsaws felling trees up the hill, so that it wasn't long before I'd made my peace with Phelps, it wasn't long before I could walk with him for hours at a stretch and come away feeling oddly refreshed.

A narcissist, he'd never tired of hearing his own voice, often discoursing at length to me about this birdsong, that archway, this antique style of hat, even waxing nostalgic, one day, about the root of some old chestnut beneath the bench where we sat, trapping the whole wide world in the net of his eye, while guiding me slowly me through the emperor's palace or São Pedro de Alcântara or (his favorite) the Imperial Museum, as when it was raining he'd had frequent occasion to do, pausing for long bouts with me before the cathedral's stained glass windows, and in the overheated museum before the trite, garish, truly silly portrait of Emperor Pedro II dressed in imperial garb delivering his Speech from the Throne, a painting that never fails to produce in me (though I fight to suppress it) the same childish urge to snicker, to snort and laugh and stamp my feet, as does Rigaud's famous portrait of Louis XIV that hangs like a pastry in the Louvre.

He'd liked to hold me there, especially there before the portrait of Dom Pedro II, and declaim at length about the noxious painting, and about Dom Pedro himself, the last Brazilian emperor, a man of genuine charm and erudition: astronomer, scholar, painter, chemist, polyglot, bibelot, reformer, disciple of Darwin and

Nietzsche, friend of Longfellow, Hugo, and Wagner, founder of libraries, schools, and universities, and zealous patron of the arts and sciences—a veritable Marcus Aurelius who must have been shamed by his wife and daughter into posing in such frippery and tights, I am sure, for I can see it in his eyes, that he detested it all, a glint, a grimace, even the mawkish, timeserving artist had known better than to betray, so that I have always had something rich in which to revel each time I was forced to stand before the silly, uproarious painting, surrounded by schoolchildren and tourists, as my rival gabbled on, inspired, insensible, descanting loudly upon the odious picture in a curious medley of Portuguese, English, German, and French, until, with a tact and discretion I have always admired in the staff there, he was pressed by a guard to move on.

In fair weather he often chose to get away from the tourists, much as he enjoyed their attention, their awe, to stray far from the busy town center, the two of us tracing a lazy circuit through the drab outer neighborhoods on foot, as the lonely Zweig himself must have done, though perhaps by different routes, sometimes with Lotte, more often alone, the two of us walking and talking, Phelps decrying at length, and at his leisure, the many feints and evasions, the shameless apocrypha, those 'solemn inaccuracies' of our many predecessors in the field, chiding Allday, Bona, Müller, and Dines, scolding Niémetz, Kerschbaumer, Rieger, and Specht, reproving even the peerless Prater, whom he hated and loved. In that way we had frequently passed the mornings when together here in town, walking and talking, and stopping here and there for coffee or beer, when often Phelps was inspired to tell me about his years as a student in London, about the people he'd met there, about the plays and paintings he'd seen, and he liked for some reason, when we were huddled together in a dreary corner of some ersatz tavern here, munching pretzels and sipping our mugs of tasteless yellow beer, to tell me scurrilous little stories about Eva Braun—how she'd preferred anal to vaginal sex, had shaved her pubic hair with Hitler's ivory-handled razor, and had liked to masturbate to the sound of highland pipes, stories he'd repeated to me without knowing it (if with subtle variations) in our many strolls throughout the city, claiming each time, as all such fablers do, that he had read them somewhere respectable or had heard them from a reliable source, so that he was willing to vouch for their integrity, their truth, though what truth they embodied he would never really say, rebuffing me with a wink before hailing the waiter for more pretzels and beer.

He'd liked the tidy German aspect of the town, a look maintained and expanded for tourists in recent years, so that it is likely the city today bears but a mocking resemblance to the town Zweig knew—larger, more crowded surely, with its Bauernfest and beer gardens, its sausages and sauerkraut, its annual parade of lederhosen and dirndls, all of which I have always found abhorrent for the gaping human emptiness it implies, that willingness to be duped and swindled, to be led by the nose, to be exploited, beguiled, abused, that eagerness to look *back* instead of *here*, to honor *then* instead of *now*, that *cultural cynicism* disguised as *cultural celebration*, all of it fueled not by genuine human pride but by *carefully manufactured pride*, which can only diminish one, every folk dance and dirndl inspired not by genuine self-respect, by a genuine love of one's customs, one's kind, but by chauvinism, ignorance, and fear, all of it disguised and exploited *as joy*, which is itself—no matter what the touts and impresarios claim—always inspired these days by profit, *if not by profit alone*, by venality, mendacity, and greed.

Now Zweig's house is scheduled to become an official part of the tourist circuit here, like the canals, the cathedral, the Imperial Museum, like the bratwurst and beer steins and dirndls. Soon his house too will appear in travel guides in a hundred different languages in a hundred different countries around the world, a place, a site—like Machu Picchu and the Western Wall, like the great mud Mosque of Djenné—that every caring, cultured person in the world must visit, must see, this modest house, the house to which had Zweig fled, the house in which he and his wife had lived and suffered and died, in which my rival Phelps has likely already been slated to speak, this house that I have watched and studied for weeks now, for years, this house before which I have seen the locals shuffle their feet and bow, before which I have laughed and spoken with the friendly young workman with the cross on his neck, this plain, unlovely little house in which I have spent every night since returning to Brazil is now scheduled to be renovated, remodeled, *renewed*, this drab little bungalow with all its secrets intact is soon to be transformed into a tasteful new museum, a gathering place for scholars, a shrine, an altar, a point of pilgrimage for the lost and lonely of the world—writers, humanists, pacifists, and Jews.

For Jews will flock here, I'm sure; they will quickly claim him as their own, as they will never claim me, I know, so that it is easy to imagine the faceless bands of tourists climbing the steep flight of steps here and pushing their way through the tiny undone house as I have seen them do at Trotsky's house in Coyoacán, where, fresh from shopping, they'd shouldered their way through the gloomy little rooms, ogling the bullet holes in the walls, examining his dingy washroom with its toothbrush and cup, and admiring his bullet-proof vest with its heavy bands of steel, while scarcely even listening to the well-intentioned, reasonably well-informed guide, a somber-looking student from the university who'd spoken with a whisper, a lisp, but gasping and gabbling over the tidy little desk at which the aged revolutionary had been working when he was killed, *assassinated*, the desk covered (as it was when he died, if without the blood, for there must have been blood) with his books and papers, with his pencils, inkpots, and pens—and there, too, his famous wire-rimmed glasses *just sitting there*, as though he'd only set them aside for a moment to rub his tired eyes, as though he was sitting there *still*, sitting right there in front of us with his unkempt hair and blazing eyes, as if still thinking, still puzzling over the proper phrasing of some trenchant, some momentous conceit, never suspecting (in the midst of our curious presence there) the presence of his assassin just behind him, never guessing, this ardent, headstrong Jew, that he would never complete his biography of Stalin, that Stalin himself would finally reach him there and *tap him on the head*, that Stalin his rival would win, never imagining (For who could imagine such a thing?) that in time his ugly, fortified house would be converted into a museum, complete with gallery, gift shop, and garden, to which tourists from all over the world would come flocking to stand by the desk where he was killed, *murdered*, to peruse his old maps, to examine his books and Dictaphone, and to admire his collection of yucca and cacti in the yard, each variety of which he himself had gathered by hand in the nearby countryside.

Of course he could never have envisioned the day when people, when tourists, pilgrims, from all over the world, would pay money (pounds and yuan and dollars, euros and kroner and yen) to see for themselves what he'd left there undone. In this, the same fashion, they will trudge their way up the steep flight of steps here, once the renovation of Zweig's house is through, they will climb it by the busload each day, each week, month after month, year after year, perhaps the very same people I saw in Coyoacán, the restless happy hordes huffing their way up the stairs with their cell phones and shopping bags, signing the handsome guestbook, gawking at the tiny rooms, admiring the tasteful exhibits (his typewriter, his pens—*Look there, his cufflinks, his wristwatch, his ring!*), watching the short, tasteful videos in Portuguese, Chinese, and English, in Arabic and Japanese, in Spanish, in German, in French, perhaps even sniffing the hydrangeas out back before taking in the view of the town and valley from the newly tiled veranda where Zweig used to work, only to snatch up their knickknacks in the little gift shop, the books they will never read, the bookmarks they will never use, the postcards they will never send but will affix to their refrigerators, and to the little cork boards above their desks, so that their friends and colleagues might see them and ask about them, when they too might feel the need to see it for themselves, the town, this house, saving up their hard-earned money and travel-ing here, to Brazil, to Rio, from Los Angeles and Cape Town and Lisbon, from Tokyo and Moscow and Rome, to drink their *caip-irinhas* and eat their *pao de quejo* and admire the holy, righteous poor—in Babilônia and Cantagalo, in Cidade de Deus—before clambering aboard one of the many air-conditioned buses that will carry them here, to this town in the mountains, the jungle, to this lonely little house on the hill in which I sit right now, this house from which I cannot help but see it all and grieve, the buses and tourists, the bratwurst and dirndls and beer.

This neglected, overgrown house, this humble cottage really, they will fit it all out with Zweig's things, his hat here, his books and papers there. And there, in the case by the door, his prized possession—Blake's portrait (now but a copy) of the mad King John! Yes they, the Friends of Zweig, the generous patrons, they will fill up this house with his things in the mindless, despicable, finally vindictive effort to reproduce his life here, an exhibit and stage show, a tidy diorama of exile, perdition, and death. They will work day and night, they will work night and day, they will call in all the experts to try to recreate his final days here, the loneliness and longing, the agony and dread, all of which they envy and fear and can only destroy by exploiting it, by packaging it and branding it and selling it like so much skin cream, like so much dish soap or beer. They will peddle it around the globe, this latest *product*, they will hawk and hustle it, they will market it with zeal, touting it widely like *haut couture*, touting it widely like *haut cuisine*, for only in that way can they defeat it, only in that way can they ever hope to neutralize its meaning, its force. They will stop at nothing to transform and betray it, this man, this house, this dark and winsome night. They will loot and ransack his life, they will pick his bones clean, they will make of him an icon, a *luxury*, they will make an idyll of his grief. For he is at their mercy, they know. They will not rest until they have turned a profit on his life, his death, until they have made it useful, *made it pay*, for I have seen it before, I have seen it a thousand times before and know that they will leave nothing to fortune, they will leave nothing to fate. They will dot every *i* and cross every *t*, they will spend every pound and dollar, every ruble and shekel and yen, to commodify and fetishize *this*, this house, this room, this last and lonely night, they

will not cease, they will not relent in their efforts to recreate the very *Geist* of Zweig in this house, in this room where he sits right now, picking at the wart on his hand, if now absently, distractedly, no longer really thinking about it at all, about his fleabites, the monkeys, the heat, nor certainly about his watch, the handsome doctor's watch with its Scottish gold dials, nor even about Lotte, his long-lost, lovelorn Lotte, about the crash and clatter of knives and forks and spoons, which he has already forgotten, sitting here in his shirtsleeves and tie, hearing only, with his heart, his eyes, the late-night tram from Rhenânia and the swirling, uncouth stars above, hearing only the tram's screeching wheels and the cold dark wind in the firmament, that whirling, swirling perfection of things he has waited his whole life to hear, and now hears as a whispering inside him, his wart, his gums, as a whispering in the dark and fecund earth, in the grubs and beetles, in the ears and entrails of the mourners at his grave who will weep their selfish tears for him, praising only the fact of their own still living, their own still breathing, for which now, all of it, they are grateful to him, and to all of the dead, everywhere at once, who burrow like worms into the dark, warm earth, the millions and millions of dead, the eons and eons of dead, all of them patiently clawing and scraping, slowly working their way toward the warm, steamy core of the earth, the nucleus, the crux, no heaven at all, but the center of things, the core, where who knows what becomes of them, only that they seek it themselves and do not fear it and *know* or seek it themselves and do not fear it and *do not know*, but trust, care less, having resigned themselves at last, digging slowly day and night, digging slowly night and day, not dreaming or feeding, no excre-
tions anymore, just a steady sloth-like scraping at the rocks and

pebbles and dirt that one can hear some nights, if one listens hard, that Zweig himself can hear tonight, here in this room where he sits on his bed in his sallow skin and sighing, in his shirtsleeves and tie. He can hear it now, with his heart and eyes, with his rootless teeth and gums, the steady sloth-like scraping of rocks and pebbles and dirt, though the night is still and the rains will not fall again until morning, a light gray drizzle that will fog up the postman's glasses when he stops at the bottom of the steep flight of steps and looks up at the house, still dark though it is morning, sorry once again that he has no mail to give them, no packages or letters or cards to deliver, no greetings from Europe, no news, not even tidings from their friends and fellow exiles in New York, wanting almost to write them a letter himself, in his own rough hand, to leave it in their mailbox, an offering, a gift, which of course he will never do, indeed is forbidden to do, which of course no longer matters now, or *yet*, for alas that morning has not yet come.

It was from my rival, Phelps, that I first got the idea of getting a look inside here, of spending a night in the house alone. Somehow he had gotten permission from the former owner, a mad, penurious woman in Rio who, knowing nothing of Zweig, of his flight from the Nazis, his death, had purchased the house some years ago with the money left her by her philandering husband, an insurance salesman who'd specialized in worker's compensation, spurred initially by the idea of renting it out, of making some easy money on it, as a poet's retreat, as a quaint mountain getaway for tourists and students and priests. She had hoped to turn a quick profit on the place, without lifting a finger, without doing a thing, but had eventually taken it off the market and closed it up, hired a workman to board up the doors and windows, then refused to discuss it at all, to even consider the many lucrative offers that had come her way, hanging up on anyone who telephoned her and enlisting the police to chase the realtors from her stoop. She had somehow been persuaded, this woman who had grown so mean, so reclusive, that even her neighbors had wished her dead, often complaining about her filthy yard and her overflowing mailbox, and about the fishlike stench at her door. This same woman, this Cândida Silveira-Villar, had somehow been convinced to give Phelps the key, to let him venture inside the long-empty house alone, which he'd done at his leisure, photographing the rooms from every angle, in daylight, at dawn and dusk, in order to compare them with the half a dozen extant photos of Zweig and Lotte in the house, stark, spectral images he was delighted to show me, all but sputtering with glee, the best of which (including two of their empty bedroom here) now appear in his book, the lot of them somehow spookier still for their particular reproduction, the paper, the sheen, the rooms shot through with a dead and murky light that seems nearly *material*, as if thick with residuum, as though indeed some essence of the lives lived there had been trapped, left suspended in the dank, long-stolid air.

By hook or crook Phelps had found his way in, when scores of others had failed, he had broken the seal on the tomb, he had entered the *sanctum sanctorum*, exploring the dank, oblivious rooms with a flashlight and camera, and meticulously recording their squalid detail, the condoms, beer cans, graffiti, and shit. He had shot it all, and from every perspective, from window to window, corner to corner, doorway to doorway, flipping every dead switch, turning every dry faucet, opening every cupboard and closet and drawer, even crawling under the sagging veranda to see what was there, there with the geckos and rats.

He had photographed it all with that restless determination of his that has finally made him his name, though he'd never found what he was after, I know, I am sure. He was never able to confirm his suspicions about Zweig, about Zweig and Lotte's death (the light, the beds, the position of their bodies, their things), qualms, conjectures, he was never quite willing to share with me, but in carefully fractured bits, which he offered up to me, in the course of our many long walks through the city, like lightly honeyed bait, speaking vaguely, obliquely, about the house and grounds, about the cook, about the gardener who had found the couple dead, and about the position of the drinking glass on the nightstand there (with its dregs of sugar water and Formicide) in which glass it had been Zweig's habit to soak his proxy teeth, and dropping a variety of names into the middle of our conversations to see what I would make of them, names like Claudio de Sousa, Sady Ferreira Barbosa, and Dr. Mario Pinheiro, mentioning them by the way, often apropos of nothing, to see how I'd react to them, if indeed I'd react to them at all, distinguishing them amidst the torrent of names that typically poured from his mouth when he talked, to which well-known names, in fact, I never responded, or rarely, if with but a chuckle or shrug, pretending, as we sat together in the somber cathedral or wandered the handsome palace grounds or finished our toast and coffee in the modest Biarritz, that I'd never heard of them or had heard of them, in fact, but had not consid-ered them significant, while knowing exactly where he was going with them, where he was leading me, but too kind, perhaps, too curious, to mock him as he deserved, grasping full well how angry and embarrassed he'd have been if I'd exposed him, if as a fellow scholar I had taken him to task, knowing surely that he'd have denied it all if I'd so much as *suggested* that he actually believed such nonsense, such things, simply biting my tongue instead, a reserve, a diffidence on my part, that had eventually paid off, so that it hadn't been long before he'd described the purported conspiracy to me in full, in grave and exhaustive detail, if with an irony that might excuse him, still eager for my reaction, as he was, to what he called *the still-mysterious circumstances of Stefan and Lotte Zweig's death*, speaking quickly, solicitously, and with a boyish conviction about the Zweigs' friend, the literato and secret Nazi sympathizer, Claudio de Sousa, who had walked and talked with Zweig just hours before his suicide, only to retail for me, with his wry, illegible grin, each of the *twenty-three discrepancies* in the official recording of their death and burial, deaths—suicides— which mysteriously had failed to warrant either an autopsy of the bodies, as was usual in such cases, or indeed any official investiga- tion of the matter at all, though the questions and inconsistences abounded, he'd attested to me at length, a neglect, an omission, recorded and decried immediately after the Zweigs' interment by respected journalist and friend, D'Almeida Vitor, who'd reported that during the wake Stefan's coffin had been left open, as is the custom in Brazil, while Lotte's had been kept closed because of the stench, the putrefaction, a fact at odds with the official finding that she had died sometime *after* her husband, *possibly hours later*, and perhaps by different means, from ingesting insecticide instead of pills, her suicide but an afterthought, a response, a reaction to his.

This and more Phelps had told me by the way, providing me,

as enticements, as clues, photograph after photograph, facsimile after facsimile, including annotated reproductions of the pages of Zweig's address book (with certain names circled, certain names crossed out), copies of his last postcards and letters, as well as a well-worn copy of his death certificate, which I had seen before, in which his name, Stefan Zweig, erroneously had been written as "Stephan Zweig; male; white; writer; parents: legitimate; married; date of death: February 23, 1942; cause of death: suicide by ingestion of toxic substance; physician who attested: Dr. Mano M. Pinheiro," none of which had ever seemed the least bit suspicious to me, the *ph* but a clerical error, nothing more, though Phelps himself was convinced of its consequence, its matter, referring to it again and again, in the course of our many encounters, only to work his way in time, as we walked and talked or sat together in the back of some gloomy German-style tavern, eating our pretzels and gulping our beer, to a fervent if well-rehearsed examination of Zweig's deathbed declaration to the world, his well-known 'Declaração,' (which—"quite unlike him, that meticulous man"—he'd actually written without the *cediha*, as 'Declaracão'), a goodbye, a farewell, I've read a dozen times before, the last two lines of which apparently had been omitted when it was printed in the local papers (indeed the lines were missing in the newsprint copy I saw), expressing as they had Zweig's dying wish for the ultimate defeat of fascism and Hitler, what poetically he'd called *the dawn after this long night*, the two lines cut out, expurgated, *bowdlerized*, so Phelps had insisted to me, his very words, shaking the paper in my face, the lines cynically, deliberately, excised by none other than their friend and confidant, the Nazi sympathizer, Claudio de Sousa, a betrayal, a perfidy, perhaps committed at the behest of none other than President Vargas himself. Who knew? Who could say?

And what about the position of their bodies, what about the bracelet, he'd pressed me one morning over breakfast at the modest Biarritz, so eager to show me the deathbed photographs again that he'd upset my coffee, staining my favorite pants, images I had seen and examined before, at least a dozen times before, but which he'd pressed me to reconsider in the light of all he'd told me, actually thrusting the folder in my face: the discrepancies, the errata, *the facts*—the best known one, from the popular paper *O DIA*, of Zweig and Lotte in a close, nearly coital embrace, captioned 'UNIDOS NA MORTE,' in which a watch or bracelet is clearly visible on her left wrist; then the one, taken shortly after, it seems, with Lotte lying side-by-side with her husband, the watch or bracelet *now missing*, her hand floating just above Zweig's own as though in the midst of patting it, though in fact only stiffened by rigor mortis; and finally the one, the official last photograph of the couple, shot from near the foot of the bed, one in which the field of vision has been increased to include not only the dead couple, the plump white pillow, and the iron headboard, but the cluttered nightstand as well, with its small reading lamp, an embroidered linen cover, a bottle of water, a rumpled handkerchief, three coins, a box of matches, and a glass, a photograph in which the position of the bodies has been altered yet again, this time, as by a painter in a *tableau mort*, with Zweig lying untroubled on his back in his shirtsleeves and tie, mouth agape as if snoring, as if exhausted from a morning spent walking or working, Lotte pressed tightly to his side, affectionately clutching his folded hands, poised—*posed*—there beside him, as if about to whisper something teasing, something playful, in his ear, as if about to rouse him from sleep, from his usual *sesta da tarde*, when they would sit in the kitchen and talk.

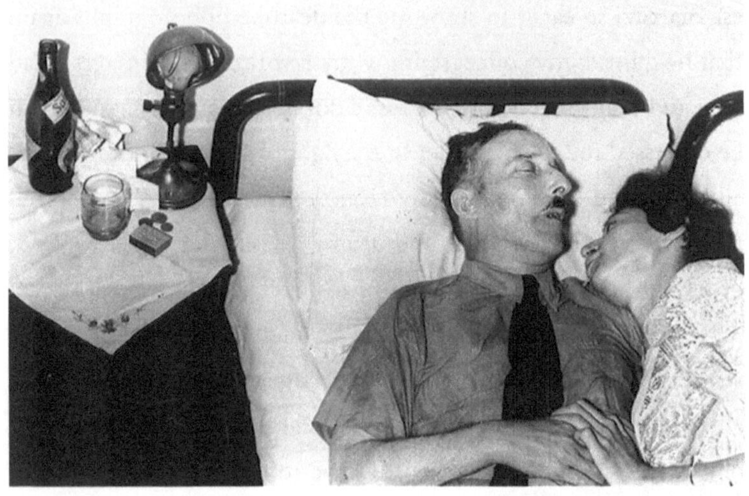

Of the three of them I like this last photo best, no matter how staged, how contrived, it may be. I like it for the way it suggests them, this Max and Carlota, this weary Adam and Eve—their innocence, their dignity, their love. It's uncanny the way it conjures them here, here and now, in this room where I sit, this room in which the night has settled hard against the windows at last, so hard that I can hear the steady, throbbing pulse of the world outside, where even now Phelps is dreaming his florid dreams, where even now you, Yaniv, are fast asleep in your bed, where even here, now, a fox stops to sniff the crates of old lettuce before the shuttered market across the street, while Lurdes, my landlady, turns over in her sleep or kicks out at the sheets and cries, perhaps sensing her fox outside, perhaps thinking of her son, of her long-dead mother as a girl in Macau. I can sense it all tonight, can feel the whole world pressing in upon this drab little house, on the walls and roof, on the pillars and windows and doors, pressing in, asserting its dominion, its weight, so that you, Yaniv, your mother, my mother, even my father is here, sitting in his car on the tracks, sitting slumped against the steering wheel in his overcoat and hat, even my father in the cold and snow in his car on the tracks is here in this house tonight, here in his Oldsmobile with the push-button gears and red leather seats. Even he is here in his car on the tracks with the snow falling down, here in this house, this room, he too is here right now in this room with me where Zweig sits alone on the edge of his bed, picking absently at the wart on his hand, hardly conscious of it at all, only wondering, thinking, the wart forgotten, the picking but a reflex now, a habit, like drumming one's fingers, like stroking one's chin. He is picking at the wart on his hand as he looks about the room with a vague, melancholy pleasure—at the chair and lamp, at the dark lowboy dresser on the top of which he considers the various items neatly arranged there on the large linen doily: his silver hairbrush and comb, the photograph of his mother, and there, amidst his tonics and pills, his tarnished bronze Shiva dancing the old world to bits. He is looking, musing, wondering idly about vain and gratuitous things, about royalties and film rights, about the maid, their little barefoot maid, and about the wrinkled brown wrapper from the wedge of Tilsit cheese. And he thinks without thinking of the dog shit in the yard, which he had meant to collect this morning and dispose of in the trashcan out back. He is thinking hard about such things, about the open suitcase beside him on the bed (into which, without thinking, he has packed his underwear and socks), about his thick English suits still on their hangers in the closet, about his mildewed shirts and ties, about his house and wife and shoes, which shoes the police will find and photograph exactly the way he will leave them to be found, lined up neatly on the floor of his closet here, with his shoe-trees and rubbers, with his trusty Fanshawe racquet now warped in its press.

When the time comes he will neatly arrange his shoes in the cramped and moldy closet here, as if still wishing to make a good impression—on the police? the neighbors? the press? On posterity itself? the thousands of tourists not yet born who will flock here with their cell phones and sandals to gawk at his books and pens, at his rubbers and racquet and shoes, who will mutter and gape at the handsomely mounted photographs of him—the celebrity, the writer, standing papers-in-hand beside his lovely, lovelorn Lotte as she types up his work; posing with Lotte on the terrace here; standing absent (one will sense him there) beside his lost and lonely Lotte in the yard. And they will wait in line, these tourists-to-come, these tourists-to-be, they will pay their money and they will push their way in to see the photographs of the two of them living, to see the two of them dead, here in this narrow bed on which Zweig now sits perspiring beside me in his shirtsleeves and tie. Even now he is thinking of this, of the bed, the future, the future, the bed, even now he is thinking of the world-to-come, not of heaven surely, nor even of karma, rebirth, but of that reckless, unmade world-to-be, so crowded with anxious, crowded people looking back that even now he can hear their wailing, their cries. He knows that they will look back at him, at this town, this house, and he'd like to know what it is they'll see. He'd like to know what is *I* see right now, what it is I find so hard to describe, to explain, piling word upon word, day after day, yet with little to speak of, to show. Why the anguish, the pain, he wants to ask me, to know, for he cannot rest until understands what it is I'm doing here now, what I'm doing here *still*, now that his story has been told and re-told, the facts weighed and sifted, his life redacted, *redeemed.*

He wants to know what more he could possibly say to me, to anyone, now when he is speechless and weary, when the night has closed in on him at last, when everything he has ever known and felt—that lush, brightly projected world—is about to collapse, go dark within him, when he has cried and protested, when he has said everything he can think of to say, no secrets anymore, when perhaps even Lotte has gotten to her feet again, the kitchen drawer on the floor where it fell (the forks and spoons and knives), when even the market across the street is closed, the women gone home, sleeping now, dreaming, when even the last tram from Rhenânia has passed the house with its empty, seashell roar.

Why now, why here, what else, what more, he wonders gravely, with what little strength he has left. To what purpose, what end? Why tell this tale *again*, he cannot guess. He cannot even rise from the bed to confront me where I sit, to demand I speak frankly to him at last, to demand, as he has every right to demand (this man with no right, no power, to demand anything at all), that I explain my presence in his house tonight, this night, every night. He doesn't even have the strength for that, poor man, but upbraids me with his eyes where he sits there on the bed, though such gestures mean nothing now, he knows, a shadow-play, another dumb show of the dead, though he is not in fact dead, not now, not yet, for surely his heart still beats, his eyes still see, his lungs still rise and fall. Surely he can still fear and remember, still laugh if he has to, still weep and count backwards from ten. He knows he is still very much alive, feels a deep quiet pity for himself, and regrets it sorely, this still-living, still striving, this limbo, this stubborn earthly pull, for such is the pressure here tonight, the longing, the dread, that he can feel it all where he sits here on the edge of his bed, the past and present, the furious, fulsome future, the walls now creaking and cringing about him, the wind soughing, the trees pitching, the fox—Lurdes' fox—sniffing the lamppost at the corner where the dogs stop to piss. So great is the pressure here tonight, so quickly has it bloomed around us in the house that suddenly I feel my head will burst from the force of it, for my tinnitus has returned, a high, unbearable shrilling, each nerve and synapse crackling with the rage of it, so that I have to curl up on the floor and close my eyes, I have to pinch my eyes shut until it passes—which at length it does, in pulses, in waves, though my mouth is chalky and dry.

It is a yipping that rouses me (How much time has passed?), a yipping that now draws me back into the world, that marks the change in the light, the dark, which is not so dark now but lighter, milky, now filmy at the edges, so that I am relieved to find that it is not too late for me to escape the house without detection, not too late for me to make it safely to the street again before the neighbors raise their blinds and rub the sleep from their eyes. By the light at the window here there is still time for me to get back to my building before the women assemble outside the little market with their net bags and coupons, with their broken-backed sandals and poorly dyed hair. I still have time, before the sun rises, to get back to my building unseen, to climb the dark, moldy stairs at the back and slip like a thief through my door, time enough, before

Lurdes wakes, to change my shirt, comb my hair, and settle myself at the kitchen table before she finds her slippers, makes the coffee, and knocks with her knock at my door.

I still have time, I know, I can tell by the traffic, the birds. I still have time before I must go, before once again I must leave Zweig here alone, here where he sits in his shirtsleeves and tie. There is still time for me to savor the simple room as it was, to admire with my fingers, my eyes, this unwonted, this *luminous*, debris—his brush and comb and mirror, on the nightstand here the lamp and handkerchief, the glass and matchbox and coins. There is still time for me to watch him pack the rest of his things, his shirts and trousers and ties, to stand with him before the small, dank closet in which he has arranged his suits and shoes, in which he has stowed his luggage, a set of three, which he purchased one winter in Rome. And there is still time for me to follow him outside, out through the wide French doors, where he likes to pace the covered terrace in the early hours, when he cannot sleep, where in the evenings he likes to entertain his friends, refugees all, his friends Feder and Fraga and Stern.

There amidst the gently clacking palms he likes to sit with them in the evenings and talk. Some nights he sits for hours in their company, the four of them, sometimes the three of them, when Fraga is busy, when Fraga is gone, talking, laughing, and smoking their cigars, their 'Havanahs', though some nights he sits alone there, after Lotte has gone to bed, after they have eaten their dinner, perhaps played a hand or two of cards, when, bothered by the insects, the hour, by the carnal haze of pollen, she has yawned her goodnight to him, sometimes kissing him on the head, the ear, sometimes wishing he would follow her to bed and kiss her, kiss her breasts, her belly, her sex, sometimes wishing there was nothing left to wish for at all.

On some such nights he likes to sit there without Lotte and her wheezing, without Lotte and her fretting, her endless worrying about the cook and gardener, about the price of charcoal and butter and meat. He likes to sit there alone, sometimes reading and thinking, often just gazing down upon the dark, narrow valley with its feebly twinkling lights, and upon the jeering fastness of the *Serro do Mar*, taking it in as one might gaze without thinking at the sky or the sea. He likes it best just to sit there without reading or writing, to gather himself up, as in a blanket, a net, though some nights he dreads his mind alone, its corners and cabinets, its windows and stairways and doors. On some such nights he is grateful to the people he knows, to Lotte, to their friends and neighbors here, to even their gruff and grumbling cook, who sometimes stays late when she is lonely, who sometimes stays late when it is windy with rain. On some such nights he is thankful for her fussing, grateful for the people he knows, stroking Lotte's hand when she is restless and feeling sick for home, teasing the dog with a sock, or chatting over pots of *chimarrão* with their friend and neighbor, the consul and poet, Mistral.

On some such nights I can actually hear their voices on the veranda outside, the fragile, soft-gabbling sounds, the two poets conversing easily, familiarly about the war, so chimerical, so distant here, about Schoenberg and Blavatsky and Freud, and about the tales of João Guimarães Rosa and Lafcadio Hearn, while Lotte, jealous Lotte, chokes and wheezes in the wings.

Some nights they are all of them here in this house at once, Zweig laughing on the veranda, Lotte coughing and wheezing in the wings. Some nights, every night, this very night now, they are gathered round him in this cramped and narrow room, though he seems hardly to notice them, to care, picking sadly at the wart on his hand, sniffing his watchband, sniffing his thumb with its fecal scent of sulfur—the books and papers he'd burned, a ridiculous gesture, he knows. The Nazis here in Brazil! *Öffne die Tür! Geben Sie sich auf!* The Nazis travelling all this way just to break down his door!

It was madness, he knows, burning his books and his papers in the yard. Even Lotte had seen it from her silence at the door, the smoke and ashes, the scraps and cinders drifting up through the trees. In his heart he knows it, this witchcraft of folly, knows by now, even now, that the Nazis have gone too far, destroyed too much, to bother with the likes of him, to care about his papers, his books. Why bother with him at all, this *rassenfremder*, this dribbling Jeremiah, this 'cadaver on leave'? Why crush his thin skull with their boots, what pleasure, what point, the punching and kicking, the stomping and smashing, why drag his remains to the street? As a message, a lesson, for whom? he wonders, for now even his death-to-be seems useless, inconsequent, moot, as even his death will stumble, fail to auger, to pray, this death that is all he has left with which to traffic, to speak, his only means by which to bring some pressure to bear on this madly spinning world, some friction, some drag. In the end what leverage does anyone have but his own dry skin, what power, what sanction, but his own haughty self-slaughter?

For we are all of us martyrs, Zweig knows, petty, pusillanimous, and vain. This he knows and fears, he has seen it before and knows. If he knows anything at all he knows that the earth will never tire of our anguish and blood, of death-made-flagrant, of death-made-merry, that history and progress are grim, spectacular, that history and progress are insatiable, gods sipping blood from the skulls of the slain.

This and more he has learned, this and more he knows—the murder of Rathenau, the Reichstag fire, the endless trainloads of the wounded and dead. Even now he can picture it, Masereel's woodcuts in *La Feuille*, can see them clearly, the skulls and crosses, the twisted wire, even here in this house, in this jungle, a million long miles from home, he knows how little (how much) is a stake, that his very pulse (he can feel it with his fingers now) is fleeting, insufficient, his life, his imprint, but a shadow on the floor, so that here, even now, he is preparing himself to be forgotten, forsaken, a gaud, a curio, some half-remembered sound, making a mental note of little things to remember, to keep to himself when he is dead and gone, when he has nothing to think of at last.

For there are so many things he would like to recall when he is dead: Rilke's sonnets, the spring in Salzburg, his first glimpse from the train of the lonely Russian steppes. He would like to remember these things, to tuck them away for safekeeping, to incise them in the very tissue of his brain—the sea at Ostend, the Blackshirts in Venice, the finely painted figures in the dome of the Teatro Colon. He would like to remember every play he has seen, every opera he has heard, the voice and handshake of every person he has met, repeating, reviewing in his mind now, the many entries in the battered old telephone book he keeps like a missal by his bed: *Richard Beer-Hoffman (Cathedral Parkway), Alfred Einstein (tel. 38-4366), Shalom Asch (tel. 3-8790, Stanford, Connecticut, Sky Meadow Drive)*. He would like to remember them all, and would if he could, if he could remember them he would, if like a schoolboy he could stand by his desk and recite the names and numbers one by one *(Rivadavia 4060, tel. 2-3555, Siegfried Berger, rua Faro 38, Apt. 202).*

Now he lurches to his feet and looks about him, as though confused, perplexed, as if baffled by the room, the light, and by the swiftly rising clamor outside. Puzzled, he touches the nightstand, touches his mustache, his chin, only to consult his watch as if to stop the earth's turning, as if to recover his position in time and space, though there is nothing it can tell him, the bright, precise ticking, such sounds mean nothing now, such restless calibrations of the wind and waters, of the uncouth moon and stars, they are nothing now, he knows, where he trembles here by the bedstead and dreads, and I am about to reach for his arm, to steady him where he stands, when—upon a blast from a car horn outside—he shimmers briefly then is gone.

❖ **February 22**

I have barely unpacked my things when Lurdes knocks at my door. She seems delighted to see me this morning, bustling her way into the kitchen as if eager to speak with me about the night, to speak with me at length, and at last, so that, as I type this at the kitchen table where I sit, I half-expect her to ask me about Zweig, about the wart on his hand, about the socks in his suitcase, about the forks and spoons and knives, it would not surprise me at all, but she starts in at once about her son, Francisco José. She is so restless, so clearly ecstatic, she can barely speak but to sputter and stammer at me, so that it is only when I have poured out the coffee and settled her in her usual place at the table here, from where she likes to peek out at the world, at her friends come shopping, at the dogs and children, at the workman with their hardhats and boots, it is only after she has lit a cigarette and puffed out her cheeks, that she is able to tell me the news. "She has asked him to marry her!" she cries aloud to me, briefly choking on her smoke. "Imagine that—*her* asking *him*! What next, I say. *Oh meu Deus*, what next, what next?"

Of course she has always loved the girl, she avers to me at once, raising her cup then banging it down again without having taken a sip. Be sure to get that down, she tells me, *peck-peck, peck-peck*, for she is determined to stake her claim in my book, to make a place for herself in this tale badly mortgaged, in this tale badly told.

And the children? Why, the children are little saints! Of course their mother has no idea how lucky she is, she declares, as if to no one, it seems, briefly rummaging around in one of the bags at her feet. Not even in Brazil do such men grow on trees. It's the Mega-Sena for her, this little miss no one from nowhere. I tell you, she lives on nothing but *farofa* and *vinho químico*! And that hair of hers! Those tattoos! But times have changed, my Francisquinho tells me, times have changed, he insists. She's an excellent mother, he swears to me, strict when she needs to be strict, kind when she needs to be kind—a heart of diamond, of gold! After all, he reminds me (just this morning he reminded me!), it was she who had pushed him to study electronics, remember, to go to night school, to get a degree, though her job pays poorly, though he himself is often tired and wants only to sit by the window and think. It is she, he reminds me each time he thinks I've forgotten it, she alone who holds him when he jerks and trembles on the floor and his tongue swells so big he can hardly breathe. It's not the neighbors then, not his cousins, his friends, not a one of them comes running, no, it is only Vitória who appears beside him when the sun blinks out in his eyes and the seas slosh and foam in his brain. It is she alone who comes to his rescue then, though she might have been out working, though she might have been shopping with friends, she alone who helps him to his feet, stroking his hair and kissing his cheeks, while her children, such willful, clever children, gently reacquaint him with his things, here your hat and coffee cup, here your cigarettes, even lighting one for him (the cocksure Clemente!) and waving it under his nose.

Where would he be without her, he often tells me, and all I can think is, where would she be without him, but that is neither here nor there, fate is fickle, it's true, we make our own beds, the pillows, the sheets, so grab your happiness where you can, I tell him. Each time he calls me I tell him that, to laugh when he can laugh and to be grateful for the little things (that are really the big things dressed up, the messiah in rags at your door: fill his cup, ask him in, and bathe his tired feet). Each time I see him I tell him that, she repeats to me, eyes hard on my fingers, *click-click, click-clack*, only to scowl and push aside the curtain to consider the commotion below, the shouting, the banging, two men unloading crates from the back of a truck, a scene she doesn't like, a scene that troubles her elation this morning, makes her crease her furrowed brow, reminding her, somehow, of the broken elevator and of the mold and litter on the stairs.

This typical morning scene makes her scowl today, makes her curse the absent landlord through the gap in her teeth, a man (once a friend) who can barely be bothered to get out his car these days but just sits there with his big fat belly and sighs. She cannot bear even the sight of him these days, let alone the sound or smell, his coughing and grunting, his cigars, though she looks forward to the day when she breaks her ankle on the stairs, she claims, as she has claimed to me before, clenching her tiny pale fists in her lap, for then, when at last the tables have been turned, when she has broken her ankle on his dark and moldy stairs, when she can no longer make it as far as the market below to buy herself milk, on that glorious day—for it will be glorious, she chirrups—she will be happy to see him again, she'll even ask him in, serve him tea, light his fat cigar, she will. And she will ask him about his droopy old wife, his kids; she will ask him about his mistress, too, the one with the anklet, the lips, why not, who cares, she is not afraid, she'll ask him straightaway about that woman in the car with him, that woman with those breasts, those lips, though he must have plenty of her kind, he must pluck them from the roadside like weeds, for such is the life he has made for himself on the backs of good people like her, she sputters, crossing herself with a vengeance, now twice.

It angers her even to think of him, she tells me as she peers at the workmen below, of the landlord, of the elevator, the mold and litter on the stairs. Despite herself she cannot help but think of it all, of his sad and droopy wife, of his snotty, feral children, of those leering red lips in the car, and swears aloud that, were it not for the fact that she has errands to run this morning, had she even a single spare minute to waste, she would telephone the fat bastard right now and give him a piece of her mind. She would pull no punches, to be sure, she would set the record straight, she declares, lips trembling, eyes bulging, but she has promised her son a new suit!

She is his mother after all, his only relation in the world, and the wedding will not wait! God forbid that anything should prevent or delay it, no, the wedding must not wait, she insists with defiance, with pride, thrusting a finger into the hot morning air, an oath, an imprecation, as if she'd declared, *the end is nigh, the end is nigh*, beat a drum for the hoof beats, cried, repent, repent, there is no more hiding, for doomsday, the rapture, is nigh, things in fact she would never have said, they would never have occurred to her, such things, they would never have entered her brightly kerchiefed head, at least so long as her son was unhappy, unwed. Such sentiments, such expressions, are not for her, I know, but for those who've shed their mortal trappings, their coupons and hair dye, their toothpaste and chocolates and rum. Such glory-eyed gossip is not for the hungry and pugnacious like her, those for whom Heaven is here and now, who worry themselves sick at night, plucking the hairs on their chin and sanding the corns on their feet. Such grim prefigurements mean nothing here, here at this table, this hour, the world-to-come in this world-that-is but a fly in her soup now, as she fingers the grimy bills in her wallet, counting them out in a language, a vulgate, I don't know, the 2s and 5s, the10s and 20s, counting them forward and backward, only to stuff them back into the folds of her shiny dragon purse.

And just as it seems she is about to rise, to set the world in motion again, (in fact she has put her hands flat on the table as if about to lever herself up from her chair), she fixes me with her small dark eyes. Yes, just about right, she murmurs, cocking her head at me where she has forced me to rise, only to jump to her feet with a tape measure in hand, barking, arms out, shoulders back, raise the waist, that's fine, while making a tangle of little signs on the back of an old receipt. Why, you could be brothers, even father and son, she cries aloud, only to pinch me lightly on the check, for she is teasing, I know, happy again to be thinking of her son, his future, his suit.

In fact she is gathering up her things now, the coffee pot, her cigarettes, her purse, eager to start the clock in earnest, to change her shoes, select a hat, powder her face, and make her way down to the street where some of her friends and acquaintances will have gathered with their dogs and children before the little market, women young and old with broken-backed sandals and poorly

dyed hair who will be quick to detect the change in her, her bear-
ing, her face. This morning they will stand offended, amazed, this
much she knows, so that she has already factored in the time it
will take her to stop and placate them, to tell them of her son's
engagement, of his wedding in São Paolo, of his reception by the
sea. And before she leaves them, before they can even close their
mouths, she will tell them about his suit, which she will stitch in a
hurry for their eyes.

So long has she waited for this day that she has already imagined them imagining *her* as she trundles her way down the street
toward town. She has already rehearsed what they will say in her
wake (some of it spiteful, much of it mean), already greeted the
hare-lipped tailor in his little shop by the courthouse and accepted
his obligatory cup of tea, a pale, kindly, scruffy old man who will
be eager to anticipate her, turning down the music behind the
counter where he sits all day at his Singer, and quickly removing
the books and samples from the chair by the door.

Every bit of it she has imagined in full, so that even before she
has turned to tell me goodbye, *até logo, até mais*, to remind me of
our dinner tonight, of the menu she has planned, she has readied
her cheek for a kiss.

Once Lurdes is gone, I wash my face and climb into bed without undressing, without even drawing the blinds, for, exhausted as
I am, I know I won't sleep.

The workmen—five or six of them—have gathered by their
trucks in front of Zweig's house. They are talking and laughing, they
are taking their time, donning their hardhats and fastening their tool
belts around their waists. Though I look for the man with the cross

on his neck I do not see him; today not a one of the men is familiar to me. What is clear is that they have come to work, whatever it was that had caused the delay now sufficiently resolved. I watch them milling about, stretching, kidding each other, kicking the curb with their steel-toed boots, until another truck pulls up beside them. It is the foreman, so much is plain, for at once they crush out their cigarettes and make respectful welcome to him, though he is clearly preoccupied, briefly examining some papers on a clipboard before tossing it—the board and papers—onto the seat of the cab.

In addressing the men he is curt, commanding. He points here and there, at the garage, at the walkway to the left, then unrolls a set of plans on the hood of his truck, which the workmen crowd around to see, grinning, frowning, nodding their heads at his instructions, the foreman himself looking up at the house now and then as if to get his bearings, even turning around to look at my building, as if to orient himself for the task at hand, before sending the workmen on their way. And at once the hammering and drilling begin. I hear shouting, clanking, the blare of a radio on the veranda. From somewhere appears a jackhammer: they are demolishing the low wall that runs the length of the sidewalk before the house. It is not the original wall.

Intrigued, I watch their progress for some time, pausing now and then to read another poem by Vallejo from the volume on my desk. The men work steadily, so that it is not long before the sidewalk in front of the house is covered with rubble. While initially it made me anxious to watch them, to listen to them talking with their hardhats and tools, it hardly troubles me now. Indeed there is something pleasing about their efforts today, about the obvious progress they've made.

I am lighting a cigarette when another, different colored truck pulls up to the curb. Two men from the electric company have arrived to speak with the foreman, whom they find in the cluttered garage, rolling out another set of plans on the hood of their truck for him, no doubt explaining where the wires lie buried, marked now by a line of tiny red flags, perhaps explaining where the new wiring will be laid, the three of them stopping now and then to point to the house itself, and to the wires overhead, all of which information appears to make sense to the foreman who shakes their hands, then waves them goodbye.

From here at my window, it is hard to determine what the workmen are doing inside the house. I hear hammering and sawing; now and then one of them passes before an open window, but that is all. Only what is happening on the veranda can I make out clearly. Two men, with chisels and hammers, are taking up the tiles from the floor there, tossing them one by one onto a heap of rubbish on the hillside below, while another man with a screwdriver removes the ugly old windows, which, along with the tiles, were installed on a budget long after Zweig's death. It will be nice to see them gone.

Now the doors to the veranda are open, so that if I squint hard I can make out the form of another worker inside the house itself, though it is impossible to tell what he is doing. Over the music I hear more shouting, this time from inside the house, something about a pipe, a drain, I think, when it is all drowned out by the rumbling of the city bus below me, as it slows to a stop at the corner with its long hydraulic hiss. An old man in a checkered shirt gets out, looks around, bewildered, then turns to the woman stepping down from the bus behind him, as if to beg her attention, to ask her something, say, the direction to the nearest pharmacy or church, but she pays him no mind, simply pushing her way past him with her bags, so that once the bus pulls away he simply stands there, looking vacantly about him and muttering darkly to himself.

He reminds me of the protagonist in Roth's short story, 'Sick People', which I read for the first time this morning. A big, lonely man, with "a vague, swaying stride," he arrives in the unnamed town "seeming to have no errand or mission." Haunted by strange images (a cell, a rickety table, a bucket that stank), he wanders the unfamiliar streets, thinking hard about the idea of order, and about the diseased world around him, standing there "in the fog of a sick world" and "grinning into the fog with rage and bitterness."

So lost, so wretched does he look, his face twisted, his pants hitched up high, that I am tempted to call down to him, where he stands frozen on the sidewalk, in fact have opened up the window to get a better look, to ensure that my voice will reach him through the din of the hammering and traffic, when I spot a workman on the hillside up beyond Zweig's house, poking around in the hydrangeas with a stick. The sight makes me gasp. What is he doing up there? What is looking for? I panic, rushing from my bedroom window to the window in the kitchen. So sick, so anxious, do I feel that I nearly call out to him, wave my arms, anything to distract him from his searching, when he pauses, bends down, only to spring upright again, holding a hammer up high. A hammer! A fucking hammer! It's enough to make me shriek with relief.

If there was any chance of sleep before there is no chance of it now. And what is sleep to me? There is simply too much to think about, simply too much to do, though for the life of me I can hardly remember what, the things I had planned, the things I must do. Thanks to Lurdes they all lie muddled in my brain, so that in my exhaustion I find myself thinking instead about the suit, the construction, the wedding. I think about Lurdes and her son, about the priest, about the reception in the restaurant by the sea. I picture Lurdes herself in her pale blue dress and hat, which she bought for herself last year, and am sorry to think that I will not be there to see her, to meet her son, his wife, to meet their children, whom I feel I remember, I know, little Abilio, dark Tisa, the cocksure Clemente. It steals upon me now, the fact that I will not be present at the wedding after all, that I will not be there with Lurdes, that I will not be there at her side, so that suddenly my work, my life, even Zweig's life, as I have trimmed and trussed it in these pages, seems but a piddling footnote to this mad old woman's dreams.

For Zweig now is everywhere and nowhere: she has scattered him like pollen, like seeds, and clucks with pleasure at my grief. Now I sense him in her voice when she sings, hear the clicking of his teeth in the trees, see his smile, that anxious, eager smile in the fine young faces in the street, for now there is nothing preposterous, there is nothing absurd, but I can imagine it here, can imagine it now, the earth so ripe today it has finally burst its mottled skin.

Such is my faith, Yaniv, that it would not surprise me if you yourself walked in through this door, drew the blinds, plumped my pillows, placed a hand on my head. It would not faze me to find you here, here in these mountains, this jungle, this town, I could make you a sandwich, we could sit here and talk, but it is Phelps instead, my former rival, Phelps, who walks in through the door and takes a measure of the room—of me in the bed, of the books on the shelves, of the papers heaped in piles and scattered on the floor, even squatting to examine a slender sheaf of them, an anguished, unfinished chapter on Zweig's old house in Bath, the house and refuge he'd bought there, during the war, after he and Lotte had fled their home in Salzburg, after he and Lotte were wed, a dark, spacious villa called Rosemount, there on Lyncombe Hill, a house to which, some years ago, Phelps and I had travelled together by train one rainy, spiteful day, before the roses had bloomed, through Reading and Swindon, the route shrouded in a chilly, phosphorescent gloom, Phelps talking all the while, doing his best to impress me—as he ate his purple sausage, as he sipped his tepid beer—with his rackety tales of the great Fielding at Twerton, of the handsome house near Bath in which he'd written his *Amelia*, in which—his triumph—he'd penned his satirical, longiloquent *Tom Jones*, speaking fervently, luridly (with so little discretion that some of the passengers had actually turned to look at us) of Fielding's affair with his little young housemaid (her tender white buttocks, her surly white breasts) and of his jaundice and asthma and gout.

By the time we'd made the journey there together Phelps had already been there before, had already explored the handsome old villa where briefly the newlywed Zweigs had lived. In the company of a local estate agent, he had toured the spacious rooms in which the couple had lived, exploring the study in which Zweig had worked, in which he'd hoarded his books and manuscripts, in which he'd hidden his Beethoven's desk, and had even descended into the damp, dark cellar, which Zweig, in his fear of a German invasion, had had stocked to the ceiling with bottles of port and claret, and with tins of dried milk and corned beef. What's more, Phelps had spoken at length with the former gardener's daughter,

Ivy, about her father's brief if poignant friendship with Zweig, in particular about the solace the world-weary writer had found there amidst her father's fruit trees and flowers, even pointing out for Phelps, there by the plum, the coarse wooden bench on which Zweig liked to sit.

It had been from there, that house, that the beleaguered exile had travelled to London each week, through the chilly English gloom, amidst the frantic preparations for war, to speak to his publisher and to visit the bank where he anxiously reckoned his accounts, every day more certain that the Germans would come. On some such day he'd had to make his way back to London through the crowds and rain to deliver a eulogy at his friend Freud's cremation at Golders Green, an occasion about which I already knew, and about which I had written at length, if ulti- mately with little intention of including the pages in my book, having described, with no particular purpose in mind, while on the hunt for other things, Freud's harried escape from Vienna in 1938, his friendship with Princess Bonaparte, and of course his cremation itself, his final defiance of ancient Jewish law, addressing myself with particular interest, indeed with a prurient fascination that has often overwhelmed my work, to the ancient Greek urn in which his ashes were sealed.

So Phelps had helped to pass the time for me that bleak spring morning, as I'd daydreamed beside him on the train, tracking my ghosts through the rain, and nodding my head whenever he turned my way, wondering all the while how I might escape him, once we arrived in Bath, how I might slip away while he wasn't looking, so as to spend the afternoon in the city alone, but he was not to be tricked, he was not to be diverted, seizing me by the arm the moment the train shuddered to a halt at the little station, and whisking me across street to the Royal Hotel for a drink.

I remember him telling me there about his plan to write a book about Primo Levi. He had already written to the author's daughter, Lisa Lorenza, from whom he was expecting a prompt and cordial reply, though his publisher hadn't liked the idea of it, another book about Levi, about the Holocaust, about his suicide in the stairwell of the building where he lived, his publisher hadn't liked it at all, complaining to Phelps about the number of good biographies on the subject already (the Thomson, the Anissimov, the Luzzatto, the Angier—*the brilliant, masterful Angier!*) and generally lamenting the glut and redundancy of such survivor stories these days, though Phelps had done his best to argue that Levi *hadn't really survived*, insisting that his plight, his story, was different, even his suicide was different. One had only to think of the years that had passed since the horror, the camps, a case Phelps had made to me in fine detail that rainy afternoon (the mail, the elevator cage, Levi's usual short-sleeved shirt), as though the decision had been mine to make, attesting to me with a tipsy indignation that given half the chance he would render the man anew, so that I was forced to play the Devil's advocate that day, to insist that his publisher was right, that it was a silly idea, that it had all been done before, and well, every row hoed, every stone turned, repeating to him, without really believing it, if with a fractious satisfaction, that the world had lost interest in such matters, such men. People only wanted to be happy these days, to hear about pop stars and billionaires, to read funny, cheerful things. It was all about the moment, the market, none of which doubts and reservations seemed to have had the slightest effect on my rival that day, as he fleshed out the stillborn project for me in all its paltry detail, a plan, a vision, in fact so deplorably conventional, so predictable, that he might have been talking about the story of *anyone*—of Pol Pot or Miles Davis or of the mad messiah, Sabbatai Zevi. So stock, so prosaic, was his pitch to me that day that I would have ignored him altogether, had it not been for the title he'd proposed for the work, *A Deep and Subtle Anguish*, a title so right, so evocative, it had all but conjured the soul-sick chemist in the flesh.

Yet even then, even with that, I'd doubted that Phelps was serious about the book, at most it was another one of his crotchets, his ploys, convinced as I was (and am) that he was mostly trying to distract me from the subject of Zweig, from the fact that we were rivals in our work, the two of us sitting there calmly, convivially, in the little bar, just minutes from the writer's old house. He had told me his idea for the book about Levi, he had hooked me with its title, not because he had had any real interest in the matter, the man, but mostly to intimidate and discourage me, to make me think that his book on Zweig was done, his visit to Bath that day just a courtesy to me. He had hoped that by telling me about his plan to write a book about Levi to make me believe that he had not only completed his biography of Zweig, but was so confident, so assured of its success, that he had already turned his attention elsewhere, to bigger, better things.

Such was the way he had often spoken to me, so that, feeling tired and contentious that day, feeling fed up with his bullying and games, I'd been unable to resist the temptation to respond to him in kind. I'd only mentioned it in passing, as we were pulling on our coats, the fact that I, too, had had my eye on Levi for some time now (Did he know that recently a cache of his letters had been found?) and was actually planning a trip to Turin that fall.

Only that had seemed to ring a bell with him, to stem his talking, to give him pause. Of course he'd laughed at me and scowled, jabbing me with his umbrella and pushing me out into the coldly drizzling rain, so that in his sudden appearance here— this spectral semblance of the man—I find a certain consolation, for though in fact his book is now finished, he himself the talk of the town, at least a part of him has found his way back here, to Petrópolis, to Brazil, to this very room in which I work. There is trouble here, he senses, there is trouble here, he knows, sniffing high and low, opening the cabinets and drawers, inspecting the ashtray, even sampling the dregs of my lime juice and rum. There is something here afoot, he can tell, he can feel it in his bones, something rising, swelling, something climbing the scales of his senses, as he prowls the room about me, something potent and troubling right under his nose.

Now his eyes flash with suspicion; he grumbles bitterly. He is so close to me I can smell him, the bug spray, the sweat. I can feel his breath on my face. Is it my weight loss, my scratching? Is it the jaundice in my eyes, he puzzles warily, so troubled by the feeling that he actually sniffs me, my hair, my clothes, sniffs my laptop, my papers, sniffs the pistol in the drawer by my knee, but it doesn't add up, it doesn't tally, it's clear, for briefly he disappears into the other room, from where at once I hear the scraping of drawers, the clatter of dishes and pans, then briefly the jangle of the radio on the shelf by the stove. He even opens the refrigerator to peer inside it, flushes the toilet, returns to the bedroom to knead my lymph nodes and feel my clammy skin, but it is all for naught, such clues leave him cold, so that at last he shakes me roughly, commanding me to look at him, to speak. What are you hiding, he demands, he exhorts me, you must tell me what you know! And suddenly he is so angry, so incensed, that he trembles with the force of it all, swelling larger and larger, where he stands by my bed, until I fear he will burst from the pressure, when like a balloon just pricked *he does*, he collapses in my chair, he surrenders, he sighs.

Or so he'd like me to think, for it's a ruse, I know, a different, more circumspect plan. I am on my guard for it, as I have seen it before, many times before. Indeed he puffs himself full again, crossing his legs and lighting one of my cigarettes from the package on the desk, which he smokes with a frigid satisfaction, now tilting his head, now adjusting his glasses, now stroking his deeply dimpled chin.

He is a handsome man, some women must love him. Surely he is not so vain, so shallow, as he seems. Now he asks me for some rum, though he doesn't like the stuff, never has, sipping it quickly, stiffly, then signaling me for more, which he doesn't touch, once I pour it, but to turn the glass to read its faded seal. For he is thinking now, devising a strategy by which to unmask me at last. In his mind he is collecting everything he knows about me, everything he has learned and gathered through the years (I picture notecards, cocktail napkins, stacks of messy files), as not even this letter to you, Yaniv, which he skims with disdain, is enough to put him at ease, so that briefly he peruses the colored spines of the books above the desk here, sampling one and then another of them (*Aus dem Leben eines Taugenichts, La Nausée*) before examining a framed reproduction, mounted on the wall by the door, of an old woodcut from 1557, a depiction of native Brazilians, cannibals, flaying and cooking a man over an open fire while some children amuse themselves with a freshly severed head, an image that makes him snort and chuckle, though clearly he is not amused by it, not really, he is not interested in the print at all, only stalling, gauging my position, my strategy, my plan, only hedging his bets, when in a voice so calm, so casual, he might be leading a seminar, he says, "It reminds me of that essay by Montaigne, you know the one, 'Of Cannibals', in particular of the passage in which he describes how they treated their prisoners of war, first supplying them with every imaginable comfort—food and drink and even women (plump, pubescent girls, if I'm not mistaken), the victors attending like servants to their prisoners' every penchant and need, feeding them and bathing them and dancing to arouse them. They did this for days, even for weeks on end, only to hack them to bits with their machetes and swords, a reversal not really a reversal at all, as indeed the prisoners expected it, *deserved* it, to be hacked to bits then eaten. Even as they fondled the girls around them, pinching their little brown nipples and probing their little pink holes, even as they scratched their balls and sighed, picking the bits of dried monkey and roasted tapir from their berry-stained teeth, they knew how it would end, that they would be killed without mercy, their parts roasted in coals then fed like sweets to those very same girls who had granted them such license, release. They knew with a faith we can scarcely imagine today that they would be stripped to their bones and devoured, the flesh, the brains, the offal, not as a form of sustenance, mind you, for the cannibals were never short of food," he adds with a languid flourish of his hand, "but merely to indicate what Montaigne called 'an uttermost vengeance'. Such an expression that—*an uttermost vengeance*, though probably little or none of it was true. The point was simply to have such stories to tell, a fact Montaigne knew well, or at least suspected, the popular tales of savages and cannibals but moral sleights-of-hand by which the purported atrocities of others were used to obscure or extenuate one's own.

"You know he was Sephardic, like you, Adam, a Marrano—accursed, a swine (the Inquisition, the monstrous Torquemada!). Not that it matters really. About such things there is no one to care these days, you've said so yourself. Still it might be food for thought were you ever to take up your pen again, a little book about Montaigne, you know, for you must have *something* in the hopper there," he prods me, indicating my laptop, my head, "some new project in the wings, perhaps a book about that writer you once mentioned to me, what was his name again...Brenner, yes, Brenner, was it Yosef or Haim, the one killed by Arabs in a riot near Tel Aviv, though I'm afraid you'd never see it in print, it's true, not these days, no, not with the way things are now," he laments vaguely, no doubt thinking of himself instead, about some project of his own, when he shakes his head and grins. "Why of course you're onto something new!" he exclaims, upsetting the books on my desk. "Yes, surely you are, for you couldn't still be thinking about Zweig—impossible, no, not after all these years, not with all now said and done. What would be the purpose, the point, why would you punish yourself that way? Surely it would be ridiculous, mad, it would be foolish, insane, all that effort, that strain. It's not possible, no.

"In any case, you'd never find a publisher for another book about Zweig, not now, not for decades to come, for the market's flush, my friend, the readers are sated, they've eaten their fill. They've belched and wiped their mouths and pushed themselves from the table. By now they've gorged themselves, their bellies ache, though they're grateful to know him, I'm sure. They're pleased to have donned his sorrows, to have eaten his heart out, to have traipsed these very streets in his shoes, so that there is nothing more they want of him now, there is nothing more they need.

"You can trust me when I tell you this, Adam, that it's time to let him go, time to throw in the towel, time to save yourself at last. Don't you see? Even his house on the hill there is mute, exhausted, it has nothing more to say. It's time to give yourself a break, my friend, to think of your future, your health. Just pack up your bags tonight, no pity, no shame, who cares about an unfinished book, it's not a book at all, not really, but a figment, a fancy, of no more substance than a whisper, a dream. Just pick up the phone there and reserve your flight home, I can do it for you, if you'd like, you deserve it, you do, this jungle, the heat, its time you got away from here, spent some time with your son. Go on, just look at your eyes, your skin, the climate doesn't suit you, the food makes you ill. For God's sake, you're not the bloody Mariner! You can wash your hands of him right now," he harries me, actually gripping me by my shirt, when adroitly he grins.

"Believe me, I know how you feel—the heartache, the strain. Why by now he must seem like an old friend to you, like a confidante, an ally—your very own Virgil in alligator shoes! *Bone of his bone and flesh of his flesh.* I know, I know! Believe me, I do. You wouldn't be the first to suffer this, far from it, hardly, not by a long shot, no. It's a syndrome really, as common as clay. Why just think of it: you've probably spent more time with Zweig than with anyone else you know, so that it's hardly surprising you find it difficult to let go of him, to turn your thoughts to other things. Think of Edel and his Joyce, of Cook and her Eleanor, of Boswell's farting Johnson. Think of Cervantes and his Quixote, of Woolf and her Mrs. Ramsey, of Kafka's Joseph K. Only think, man, think! Think of Fedya's Raskolnikov, of Lowry's Fermin, of billowing Bellow's own Chicago Tom Jones. It's time to give him up, I tell you! Think of Richardson's Clarissa, of Melville's Ahab, of Bernhard's brilliant black sheep, Murau. Don't you see, they had to let them go! Consider Fuentes, poor Fuentes—his Christopher unbroken, his Christopher unborn? And what about Proust? Why the great Proust could never make the break, they had to pry the pen from his grip! And so it goes, and so it must be. Only think of Zweig himself, that restless hunter of souls. Think of his 'Master Builders': his Erasmus, his Dickens, his Kleist? Think of his Tolstoy, his Nietzsche. Think of his Marie Antoinette. Why, he must have reeked of her some days!

"Yes, I can see it in your eyes, my friend, you too have felt the bite, the sting, you have woken amazed to find yourself in Zweig's own pajamas, in Zweig's own skin, feeling with his finger-tips, thinking with his brain, appraising what is left of his world through his own mournful eyes. *The delirium of the depths*—believe me I know! I have gladly lost my way, but you... (here he hesitates, stabs a finger at my chest) you are *you* and can never save him, you know. Trust me when I tell you, you will never set him free.

"Of course I envy you, I do," he adds insouciantly, making a show of examining his nails, which he has clipped and filed with care. "And I pity you, too, for he has hollowed you out, devoured your entrails, your bones, a cannibal, an incubus really, the sort you read about in books. "Have a look there," he exhorts me blithely, indicating the mirror by the door, mark the change for yourself, when in his impatience, he explodes, "You fool, you owe him nothing, can't you see what he's done?"

He is right: I hardly recognize myself and stumble to the kitchen for some aspirin to relieve my aching head.

Across the way more trucks have arrived. Three men have gathered on the roof of the house and are now examining the crooked television antennae and pulling up some of the rotten shingles.

The work on the veranda continues apace, the windows now gone. Only the rusted white casement remains. Below the house, at the base of the short driveway, a workman is shoveling sand into the mouth of a cement mixer, stopping occasionally to add some water from a hose. Some children, boys mostly, have gathered on the sidewalk there to watch the men. The foreman has brought in a bobcat and driver who is hard a work now clearing a path along the wall that skirts the back of the restaurant next door to the house, tearing up the ferns and hydrangeas, and even toppling a large banana palm. I have seen the plans: it is where the new flight of steps is to go.

Not long after I arrived here this time, I made an appointment with a clerk in the city office to look at the plans for the renovation of the house. I'd told him I was a neighbor, that I worked at home, in an apartment across the street from the site, and was concerned about the certain increase in noise and traffic and dust, even going so far as to inform him that I'd recently been hospitalized when my esophagus closed shut.

Of course he'd been deeply sympathetic, had fetched me a glass of water, and, out of deference to my ailment (he was clearly troubled by my appearance, by the pallor of my eyes, my skin), had spoken so softly to me that I'd had to strain my ears to grasp what he'd said.

In any case he had shown me the plans I'd requested, had left me alone with them in the small conference room overlooking a neglected garden there for the better part of an hour, no doubt distracted by other tasks.

The plans themselves had meant little to me, for I'd known they were for naught. What I'd wanted mostly was to confirm my suspicion about them. And so I had, slipping out by the back stairs without troubling the kindly young clerk.

Now I look about the apartment; there is plenty to do before I go. The table is filthy, the sink full of dishes, and I begin at once to set things to rights, clearing the table, pushing in the chairs, emptying the ashtrays, and bundling up the newspapers and magazines to carry to the trash bin downstairs.

The woman who cleaned the place had died shortly before my arrival, something about her heart, and Lurdes had never gotten around to replacing her, so that now every surface in the apartment is covered with a pearly haze of dust. I work avidly, numbly, carried away by the prosy rhythm of the work, dusting and scrubbing, sweeping and mopping, wiping the windows, the toilet, the tub, even beating the rugs in the parking lot out back, so that it is nearly four o'clock by the time I am through.

All told, I am pleased with the results: the kitchen sparkles, the dishwasher is loaded, the refrigerator is humming and clean. In the bedroom I have swept up the dead moths, changed the sheets and pillow cases, dusted the bookshelves, and cleared off the little desk at which, for weeks now, I have sat like a scrivener at work. All that remains is to pack up my things.

I begin with my books and shoes, arranging them neatly in the bottom of my large leather suitcase, my Benjamin, Zweig, and Ficowski, my Steiner, my Citati, my Arendt. Instinctively I sniff my old paperback edition of *In Praise of Folly*, tucking it with care between a pair of canvas shoes.

Bleary, exhausted, I rinse my face with cold water in the bathroom sink, only to return to the bedroom where I empty the suitcase onto the bed. The moths have eaten a hole in one of my shirts; I hadn't noticed it before. I check my other shirts, my shorts, and underwear, my socks, before arranging them neatly in the suitcase again.

Why I trifle with these things, why I gather up my books, why I bother to fold my pants and shirts, I cannot say, but there is something about them, their solidity, their simple *hereness* now, that I find reassuring. There is something about the fact that I can know them by sight, by touch, that makes them seem real to me, that makes me seem real to myself, so that once I have packed them, once I am satisfied with the job, I pack them again, rearranging the items in a host of different ways, only to restore them to their original places, before testing that the suitcase will close.

It is not at all like taking a trip, no waiting, no taxis, no checking for passports and tickets, no fumbling for credit cards and cash. One needn't rise early, bring the cat to the neighbor's, set the timer for the lights. One needn't speak to the postman at all but just open the door and go—which reminds me of the keys, Fernão's keys, which I'll leave for Lurdes this evening on the stand by the door. For there'll be no fiddling with the lock tonight; I will not even say goodnight, goodbye, but slip away without a whisper, a word, making my way down the poorly lit stairs and pushing my way out into the street where, depending on my mood, I might stop to laugh with the women there, to exchange some pleasantries, to grumble idly about the corruption, the traffic, the heat. I might take one last turn through the little market downstairs, fill a cart with my favorite things. I might chat with one of the girls at the register, the one with the ring in her nose, might ask her what she thinks of the melons out front, what she thinks of the future, of fate.

Or I might say nothing to her at all, who knows, she might not even be working tonight, I might find her mother there instead, a buxom, high-haired woman who likes to tease me when she can, mocking my accent and pinching my skin.

If I'm feeling alright, I might chat with her a while. She is funny, she is lonely, I know, for her husband tends the meats there, chopping and carving all day. I know that some days she can barely stand to look at him, his raw red ears, his blistered red neck, though he is kind enough to me, his apron stained with blood, his hands chilled from the freezer in which he works. He likes to show me his favorite cuts.

It would be enough if they could just see me before I go, perhaps chat with me a while, such is the funny way I feel right now. If I could ask them about a coupon, a price, if, with my body, my cart, I could hold a place in the line—surely that would make me happy, surely that would be sufficient, enough.

Or I might not bother with them at all, the girl, her mother, the lightly marbled meats, I might not visit the market after all, but sit for a drink in the restaurant on the corner here where people will jostle me and talk.

It will be crowded by then, perhaps there'll be some locals I know, what's the hurry after all? I might chat with the waiters, I might buy old Gino, the bartender, a drink. Or if the place is too crowded, if I cannot find a place at the bar, I might sit for a while by the canal, though the water sometimes reeks. I might sit by the canal, I might stroll peacefully beside it, admiring the deep night sky through the heavy-hanging trees, for I have grown to like this city, this town.

I'd like to think I'll miss it, that I'll remember such things, the deep night sky, the people, the heavy-hanging trees. I like to think that I'll remember something, anything at all, for it seems impossible, abominable, that death should be so total, autarkic, complete. Surely some vestige of one's life must outlive this mortal coil, surely something must endure, if but a puddle of disparate yearnings, if but a glimpse, a pinwheel, of light. Surely it has not been for nothing, this life, but there must survive within one a relic, a memento, some viaticum on which to feed, a simple token to press to one's lips, to trouble in the darkness like a scarab, a bead.

Hear me, Yaniv, when I tell you I would give anything to remember you forever, though you had cursed and forsaken me, though you had cut me from your heart. For it is better to remember than to be remembered. Zweig himself knew this well, so that here, as he wandered the streets here alone, as he sat with a book on his veranda at night, slapping at the mosquitoes, chafing at the dampness, the heat, he would have sacrificed every bit of his fame, I know, he would have forsaken his dearest, most faithful friends, he would have burned his precious manuscripts, his Bach and Haydn, his Locke and Hitler, his Beethoven, Goethe, and Freud, he would have dumped them in the street—anything at all *to remember*, to recall forever a voice, a face, any face at all, a handshake, a poem, a grin.

Yaniv, were I granted one wish I would choose to picture your face forever, to hear your laughter, your humming, your tiny footsteps in the hall… I want the crack in the tea-cup to open to the land of the living instead, for I'll have no patience for the darkness, I'll have no patience for the dead, but stand forever with my eyes to the wall, so that the only thing that saves me now is the thought that you might read this someday, that one day, when you are older, when you are working and married, when you have children of your own, your aunt, who has never despised me, will share this letter with you. She is alive with such mercies, I know.

Now Lurdes is banging at my door, she is overloaded with satchels and bags, she is cursing the broken elevator, the heat, she is cursing these days without reason or rain. She cannot find her keys, she clamors aloud to me, gesturing frantically at the lamp by the couch. There, there in the drawer, she commands me, but I am not quick enough, so that she pushes past me, grumbling, never mind, take these bags, I'll get the keys myself.

Her brother worries about the way she forgets things, she tells me now, flopping down in one of the soft leather chairs by the sofa, to which her skin always sticks. The truth is that she remembers too much, she insists to me, adjusting her bag on her lap, which is why she forgets things in the first place—her keys, her wallet, the appointments for her teeth. Anymore these days she remembers too much and too well.

Her face is flushed, her upper lip damp with sweat, and for a moment she closes her eyes, inhaling sharply through her nose, only to release the breath in spurts.

She has been to the hospital today, the one up the hill here,

Beneficência Portuguesa, to visit with her friend, Fedelcina, who sits at the desk by the entrance all day, and to see about the washing there, the smocks and sheets and pillow cases, which she sometimes agrees to do, stuffing it into the mouths of the large old machines in the basement, when the staff is too busy, perhaps short-handed, when some member of the staff is ill, though she never got around to asking about the laundry today, she informs me, by the way. Instead she spent her time there, in the crowded lobby, patients hacking, groaning, doctors talking on their cell phones, nurses tapping their charts with their pens, telling her friend about her son's wedding, the music, the food, and about her son's new suit, describing for her the goggling variety of cuts, the English and Italian, the American, the German, the French.

They—Lurdes and the tailor—had talked all morning of fabric and buttons, of pockets and lapels, of patterned linings, nipped waists, and padded shoulders. He had shown her so many photographs and illustrations, she had sipped so many cups of tea, she had fingered so many swatches of cloth, that by the end it had made her dizzy to think of them and she'd had to close her eyes just to think.

Yet now the job was done; she'd bought her son a suit, she exclaims to me with pride, as surely she'd exclaimed it to her friend Fedelcina this morning. Happy, exhausted, she is about to rise from the chair, she has cooking to do, when abruptly she considers me where I'm standing at the window.

She can see the house from there, I know. She is looking at Zweig's old house across the street. She is looking at me and she is looking at the house, the house in which Zweig and Lotte lived, the house in which Zweig and Lotte died. I don't even have to turn my head to know that she is looking at it, that she is imagining the empty rooms inside it, peering in through the dirty windows, pacing the terrace, cursing the hydrangeas in the yard. I can see it in her fingers, the way they twitch, I can see it her eyes, when suddenly she is clucking about the suit again, about the tailor's grumpy wife, finally gathering up her bags with my assistance and stumbling her way out the door.

I walk her as far as her kitchen table, upon which she thumps down the cheap plastic bags, one of which has torn in her hands, so that a can of soup rolls off to the floor.

The yellow walls of her kitchen seem nearly liquid in the languid evening light, though she doesn't like the color anymore. In fact the wall by the stove is covered with the brightly painted chips she's collected from the local hardware store, commercial samples of paint. Years ago she'd taped them there to see if any of the colors would speak to her, but she still can't decide, can't make up her mind, so why bother now, she'd asked me the other day. She's grown used to the chips themselves, hardly sees them at all, except in the deeper parts of her brain, a phenomenon she called *caritas*, clearly having misunderstood the term, yet linking the words color and charity in my mind in a way I now associate with this particular shade of yellow, and with her patchwork of brightly colored chips.

She shows me the pineapple she bought downstairs, has me feel it, sniff it, then cut it up, as she has taught me to do, slicing off the crown and base, removing the skin in narrow strips, then gently scooping out the small black eyes. She likes it sliced rather than chopped, she thinks it prettier, and isn't presentation half the taste, she reminds me, as if doubting it herself, only to shrug her padded shoulders and sigh. Anyway it's what the Japanese say, she tells me, meaning it's what her dentist Dr. Soga says. He is always trying to take her out for sushi, though she's never been tempted, the raw fish, his tiny hands and feet, she has never liked octopus or squid, and who is he to think she would or *should*, just because he drives a little sports car, just because he cleans and drills her teeth. He knows nothing about her, about the suit she just ordered, about the wedding, her son, though he's been to Macau, to the very street where her mother once lived. For he likes to travel, her dentist, to gamble a bit when he can, though since his wife died he can gamble whenever he likes, he can gamble whenever he see fit, something she doesn't care to hear about, to know, though she likes it when he speaks of Macau, the island where her mother was born, sometimes stopping the drill to tell her more.

Once he brought her a hand-carved Fatima from St. Domingo's church, the church in which her mother was christened, a rustic likeness which she has never thrown away, which she keeps on the nightstand by her bed, for she is not a spiteful woman. In her way she is grateful to him, sometimes kissing the little statue before switching off the light.

She hasn't the time for ill-will these days, she often tells me. It consumes one really, sets up house, soils the bedclothes, eats up the chicken and rice. Better to turn the other cheek, she thinks, forgive when one can, for who can say how the rewards of Heaven are meted out? Who knows what goodness actually looks like, we might be very well surprised, some devil on the throne in our steads. After all who are we to know anything of Him; always He confounds us, He humbles and confuses us, He triumphs, He must. Why, we don't even have the tools to pick His teeth, she quips merrily to me, as she puts away the onions, the milk.

From such items it is impossible to deduce what she is planning to make for me, what she will prepare for our dinner tonight. She loves the mystery of such things, she loves my confusion, and now presses me out the door, locking it behind me with a bumptious rattle and click.

There is nothing for me to do now but read or write. Excited, strangely happy, I light a cigarette and sip a little rum at the kitchen table from where I can listen to the housewives and children below.

Across the way the workmen are still at it, and briefly I am tempted to venture more closely, eager as I am to see what they've done. I imagine slipping in through the gate they've left ajar at the foot of the driveway, skirting the trucks, the wheelbarrows and trenchers, clambering round the heaps of rubbish, the bricks and tiles, the tangled wire, the chunks of moldy plaster, before hoisting myself up onto the ivy-covered wall. From there it would be easy to reach the veranda, to scale the parapet and let myself in.

I could tell them I'm an inspector, for they'd be startled to see me, I'm sure. I could tell them I'm a writer for a foreign press, would they mind if I looked around. I would promise them any-thing, I'd wear a helmet, I'd ask no questions, I'd stay out of their way. And perhaps, when they'd finished for the day, they would offer me a beer, for it would be late, the foreman gone, such men they always drink beer. Patting the dust from their jeans, they would ask me where I'm from, this accent of mine, they would ask me why I've come, when, if they were not in a hurry to pack up, to get home to their girlfriends, their children, their wives, I would tell them everything about me, about my illness, my teaching, my work. Of course I would tell them about you. And I would tell them about this little house that I've been studying for weeks now, for years, this house that they have stripped to its bones, this ugly, bashful little house with its rusted pipes and broken windows, with its naked headers, rafters, and joists. I would tell them all about it, guiding them at length and with pleasure through the tiny rooms, through the living room and dining room and pantry, with their stacks of tiles and cans of paint, and through the dank little kitchen in which the Zweig's barefoot maid used to sing. And perhaps, if they seemed ready, if they were not impatient to go, I would tell them about Lotte herself, the lonely, lovelorn Lotte, about her beauty and her asthma, when at last I would tell them about Zweig, the man, the writer, the subject of my work. I would tell them about his celebrity in Europe, about the rise of fascism, about the fervid public burning of his books, when, if they were willing, I would tell them about the war, about Hitler and his rallies, about his faithful *Sturmabteilungen* and *Schutzstaffel*, the dreaded SA and SS. To set the scene, I would tell them about the *Anschluss*, the Nazi invasion of Austria, and about the desperate flight of its Jews. Sipping my beer, I would unravel the tale slowly for them, speaking first of Vienna, of its cafés and nightclubs, of the music and dancing and theatre, then of Himmler and Goebbels, then of Stangl and Goering, and Hess. And I would tell them about Eichmann, about his escape and hiding, about his eventual capture in Buenos Aires by the dogged and fearless *Nokmim*. Seated there on the veranda with them, I would tell them all about the secret operation to bring him to justice at last, about the months of deliberation and planning, the spying, the forged papers, the getaway cars and decoys, the rehearsals, the disguises, the setbacks, the pains, when, lifting my arm and pointing to the spot so they could see it, I would tell them of Eichmann's scar, of the SS tattoo he'd had cut from his flesh. I would tell them about how, once captured, once secured, he'd been smuggled out of the country under cover of night, about his lengthy trial in Jerusalem, and about his death by hanging at the prison in Ramla. I would tell them this, and I would tell them about his cremation that very same day, how, out of a fear he'd be martyred in the years to come, his body had been burned to ashes, the ashes loaded aboard a Navy patrol boat, then dumped like so much chum in the sea.

On my laptop I would show them what Eichmann, what the Nazis, had wrought, black and white photos of the cattle cars and corpses, of the heaps of empty canisters of the pesticide, Zyklon-B. Only then, if they were still listening, would I show them pictures of Zweig himself, of Zweig here in Brazil, signing books at a shop in Leblon, at the beach in Ipanema, at his desk in the Hotel Paysandu, where he and Lotte lived when they first came to stay.

Now look, I'd press them at last, pointing to the image on my screen, that's Lotte, that's Zweig. See those pillars there? That's *these* pillars *here*! Look closely, it's true. It's where we're sitting right now!

I would tell them that and more. If I could I would render
Zweig and Lotte in the flesh there before them, I would reproduce them wholly, so that the workmen would know them as they
were on the terrace that day, that bright and fragile day, as they
smiled and chatted before the camera, the cook admiring them
from the doorway, the tram clanging its way down the hill behind
them, their little dog Plucky frisking and yipping at their feet.
And for the men who remained I would conjure the lonely couple
in their bedroom there, on that warm and fateful night, I would
recreate them—sinew, muscle, and soul. I would reproduce their
every scent and expression, the furtive smiles, the breathing, the
fumbling, the sweat, I would paint the very grief in their eyes, as
they removed their shoes, as they swallowed their pills and sighed,
finally settling themselves together in one of the hard narrow beds.
Then for a time we would watch them without speaking, a fly
buzzing drowsily against the windowpanes, the faucet dripping in
the little basin there, the poem by Camões tacked like a flag to the
wall by their heads:

> *No mar, tanta tormenta e tanto damno;*
> *Tantas Vezes a morte aperecibida!*
> *Na terra, tanta Guerra, tanta engano,*
> *Tanta necessidade aborrecida!*
> *Onde pode acolher-se um fraco humano?!*
> *Onde terá degura a curta vida,*
> *Que não se arme e se indigne o céu sereno*
> *Contra um bicho da terra tão pequeno?!*

And if we were patient, if we listened long enough, when their
limbs had stopped twitching, when finally their breathing had

ceased, their lips gone dry, their lips and nails turned blue, we would hear the rising clamor of the birds outside, see the light change, hear the cook in the kitchen as she prepared their breakfast for them at the little table there, their eggs and coffee, perhaps a plate of sliced papaya, and also—always—a jar of *requeijão*, the plain white cheese they liked to spread on their toast.

And soon she'd be knocking at their door, rattling the doorknob, calling firmly, then anxiously, finally crying aloud. We'd hear voices below the window outside, muffled talking, the gardener and his wife, the terrier, Plucky, barking beside them in the yard, followed shortly by the thump of a ladder against the side of the house. And soon the moment would come: we'd hear the scraping of tiles on the roof, see the gardener looking in.

Now I consider the women who have gathered here on the sidewalk below. Most of them are familiar to me—their tight shorts and shirts, their cheap plastic scandals, their bloated arms and breasts. Surely I will miss them, their kidding, their singing, the shrieks of laughter, relief. Even the sluggish city bus that stops before the corner here with its long hydraulic hiss—I will miss that too, a bus for which I have often stood waiting, a bus which I have often taken into town when feeling restless or lonely, when eager for new faces, new sounds, enjoying its sluggish course along Rua Washington Luis, with its flagrant azaleas, regal palms, and dazzling bougainvillea, to the crowded city center, to the palace and cathedral, to the exhibits and gardens of the Imperial Museum, sometimes heading straight for my favorite bookshop or cafe, or for one of the many antique shops there in which I like to browse through their collections of prints and old maps, sometimes just sitting for a while amidst the milling tourists in the Santos Dumont house, where the docent and ticket-taker knows me, soothed by his high, bright voice, and by his curious way of bowing before the little glass cases as he talks, as if to disavow what he's said. Sometimes I don't get off of the bus at all, content just to behold the commotion from where I sit behind the large tinted windows, the touts and vendors, the clowns and musicians, the brightly dressed tourists with their cameras and hats, occasionally chatting with the driver, occasionally changing my seat as the bus loops back toward Valparaíso, when I can sit where I like.

Sometimes when I'm tired, when I feel too restless to work, to read, pacing the tiny rooms here until I feel I'll go mad, I take the first bus I find at the busy central station in town. I never look at the head sign but clamber aboard the crowded coach, paying my fare and tramping my way to a seat near the rear.

My fellow travelers are usually the same, not the same people, mind you, as the buses I take vary greatly in their routes, but the same sort, the same type—salesman, local farmers and ranch hands, and always a variety of young domestic workers, women mostly, returning to the towns where they live.

In the past weeks I've taken the bus to Magé and Itaboraí, and to the crowded beach at Saquarema where, drunk and barefoot, I cut my heel on some glass. And I have taken the bus north through the mountains—a sickening, startling ride—to Nova Friburgo and Bom Jardim, as far as Aperibé and Bom Jesus do Itabapoana, where I spent the evening drinking rum and watching television in a modest, family-run hotel on a short and treeless street, before tossing and turning in the hard, narrow bed, haunted, from the bus ride, by the snarling sound of chainsaws and by the acrid smell of smoke, while dreaming vastly, sadly, of *quilombos*, the deep jungle hideouts of runaway slaves. Had I not been awakened the next morning by a splitting headache, I might have travelled further still—to paddle the Amazon, to see an opera in Manaus, who knows, why not? Or I might have journeyed in a different direction altogether, to Belo Horizonte, to Brasília, that make-believe city I have long wished to see.

The city bus now hisses to a stop below my window. There is scarcely anyone inside it tonight, a pair of teenagers, lovers surely, and a woman with a hunchbacked boy, maybe eight or nine, dressed smartly in a brown leather vest, red neckerchief, and black cowboy hat, the sight of whom reminds me of the Marxist, Gramsci, who was born with a kink in his spine that the doctors had tried to cure by having him suspended from the ceiling for hours at a stretch. Gazing down at the bus, I picture the little cowboy suspended from the ceiling in a large leather stirrup, hat on, hat off, while his mother stirs a pot at the stove.

He doesn't see me, the boy, pointing out the window where he sits and proudly adjusting his oversized hat. He doesn't see me here, in my apartment, where I sit looking down at him and his grandmother, and at the lovers just behind them. The girl has draped her skinny legs over his, she is reading the lines on his hand. They are laughing, the house on the hill beyond them now an eerie, moonish blue. They are laughing and taking advantage of the nearly empty bus to sniff and fondle each other. I see his hand on her small left breast, which she makes a show of clutching coyly, twisting back his fingers, only to bury her face in his neck as the bus pulls away from the curb, and for a time I do my best to follow them in my mind, the lovers, the old woman and the hunchbacked boy, imagining the people who will clamber aboard at each subsequent stop, as I have seen them clamber aboard it before, mostly teenagers at this hour, acolytes of love who have bathed and dressed and combed their hair, who have waited all day for this night, so that soon the bus will be crowded with them, with their music and laughter, with their all-too-ardent scents, all of which I can only imagine from here, for now even the whine of the bus itself is gone, has faded away, been absorbed by the hum of traffic at the foot of the hill and by the music from the restaurant across the way, which now swells up in the dank evening air, as if to fill the sudden vacuum, the music and voices from the patio growing steadily louder, the neighbor children squabbling next door, the proud and lonely housewives shouting and laughing and teasing each other before the market downstairs.

From across the street I can hear the few remaining workmen still hammering away inside Zweig's house, see their trouble-lights inside, and, from above the house itself, the rising, raucous chatter of monkeys in the trees. A telephone rings, the pipes gurgle in the wall by my head, when there comes the familiar clatter of pots and pans from the apartment next door.

Lurdes is talking to herself or to someone on the phone, it is often hard to tell. Some nights she talks and laughs as if sipping rum with a friend, as if giddy, untroubled by the world, as if giddy, untroubled by her son, and some nights, when our windows are open, I can make out the sound of her sniffling, her voice plaintive, wistful, sick, as if her late husband was there in the room with her, there in the flesh, stroking her hair or patting her hand, as though he'd returned just to tidy up the kitchen after dinner, to wipe down the table, to take out the bottles, the trash. Perhaps he has only called her on the phone, having dialed the numbers with his thick invisible fingers, who knows? So faint, so ghostly is her voice on such nights that I can rarely distinguish her words, which seem less like words than luminous clusters of sound that rise in the heat and then burst.

Yet tonight she is happy, I can hear it in her pots and pans. Indeed it isn't long before my stomach starts to grumble at the strange, if pleasing smells—soy sauce, maybe pork ribs, maybe *minchee* with rice, but then I smell the coconut milk and curry: she is making *galinha* à *portuguesa* tonight, her mother's favorite dish, a dish she has promised to make me ever since we met, when, drawn to her apartment by the aroma one day, I found her preparing it for a friend of hers, a widow downstairs, though there is actually nothing Portuguese about the dish, nothing at all, she'd insisted to me, as a matter of record, as a matter of course, briefly opening the oven door for me so that I could sniff it, nor Brazilian surely, it comes from India, from Goa, she'd explained without my asking, brought by traders to Macao where her mother's mother had made it every Sunday for their meal after church. Even straight through the war she'd prepared it without fail, though she'd sometimes used roosters instead, for they are just as good when baked all day, a remark, a recollection, that had moved her to show me a small, framed picture she keeps on the wall by her bed, a simple ink drawing of the old Ah-Ma Temple there, with its ugly stone sentries, a pair of chicken-like dogs, a centuries-old shrine dedicated to the venerable Ma-tsu, the goddess of fishermen and sailors, who, according to legend, died of exhaustion after swimming out into the bay one night to rescue her father, a fisherman caught in a storm, and who has never rested since, roaming the seas of the world in a bright red dress.

Since then, since that first occasion, Lurdes has occasionally shown me the drawing, which her mother had brought with her to Brazil, sometimes chuckling at the ugly dogs, sometimes musing, reminiscing, sometimes sitting silent beside me, not stirring, scarcely making a sound, only gazing at the picture in my presence, pleased by the silent company of my eyes, by the fact that we were looking at the same thing, the same tree, the same steps, the same skinny old vendor with his wide, flat baskets of egg tarts and almond cakes, which she has long supposed him to be selling, though from the picture it is hard if not impossible to tell.

Ever since she was a girl, when her mother kept the drawing on the nightstand by her bed, she has imagined the special taste of the tarts the man is selling there, outside the temple, has imagined sitting with her mother and brother on the warm stone steps, a breeze blowing off the water, the smell of incense in their clothes and hair. Over and over she has pictured the scene: the three of them sitting there, enjoying the little tarts her mother called *pastéis de nata* before making their way home along the narrow cobblestone streets to where the coolness of the large, shuttered rooms is rivaled only by the muffled footfalls of servants and by the gentle plashing of a fountain in the courtyard below, though such details are nothing she herself remembers, they are nothing she herself has seen, has known, the tarts, the temple, the cool, dark rooms. For all of her dreaming she has never been to Macao, she has never even left Brazil, as she has often lamented to me. Such details she remembers only vicariously, having gradually (by a means she could never explain) grafted a branch of her mother's oft-told memories onto the slender trunk of her own, which over time and with careful tending has produced but a handful of tiny, bitter-tasting fruits, the flavor of which she's grown used to, she claims, is now fond of, it seems, squinting at the little picture and smacking her freckled lips.

By the clock on the wall it is 6:22: the sun has nearly set. As ever at this hour the sky is filled with bats. No doubt a walk would do me good, and briefly I picture the routes I might take, wandering down along the canal, perhaps making my way up the hill here past my favorite restaurant, *Le Petit Poulet*, but I'm not in the mood for it, for the noise and tumult below, for the women gathered before the little market here, who will look at me and whisper, who will look at me and *know*.

In any case it is too hot, too humid, to do anything but sit here and think, for the heat hangs heavily in the street here this evening, the asphalt, the traffic, the fumes, even the trees on the hill above Zweig's' house seem wasted, spent, their branches drooping, their leaves and blossoms now withered and dry.

It has rained only once since I've been here, only once in five weeks, a brief sprinkling in the vacant, early hours of dawn, when, exhausted, I'd wandered out onto Zweig's veranda, into the gray, crepuscular light, extending a hand to feel it, the rain, I'd actually stuck out my tongue, listening without breathing to its lonely patter on the wide, ribbed leaves, a sound, like that of the sea, that must have filled Zweig with grief, so often did he hear it, so surely would the jungle grow when he was dead, when Europe had vanished, when Vienna was but ashes and smoke, the twisted lianas, the epiphytes and bromeliads, the ubiquitous walking palms. There must have been times when he thought he heard the growth itself, the creaking and soughing, the whispering of grasses, the stealthy advance of lichen and moss. Some nights, when it was still, when he was lying weary and restless in bed, perhaps awakened by Lotte's wheezing, perhaps awakened by the rain, he must have sworn he heard the very mold in the fibers of his suits, the twitching of its tiny hairs, the hungry clamoring of its innumerable, inexorable spores. For there can be no God when the rains fall here, no pattern, no plan, Zweig's life no more a schema, a symbol, than mine—but a knocking in the darkness, *a stumbling about amidst great dim intimations*: the collapse of a bridge, the eager witnesses, the spring within the spring!

What at this point can I say about the man? What at this point can I say about *me*? Describing myself, describing this man, this *mass of matter and passions*, is not like removing the back of a watch to uncover the parts inside. People do that every day and still know nothing of Time. Heart and lungs, muscles and tendons, blood and bones and brain, they are not enough to make a woman, a man, not enough to rouse the mumpish dead. What escapes us is all, the mystery, the whole. Zweig's shoe size, his favorite opera, the brand of toothpaste he used—but details, mere data, so much minutiae without meaning. The songs his nanny sang him, the color ink he used, even his letters and novels and plays—such shards they tell us little or nothing, we know, though we gather them like diamonds, though we gather them like sticks. On the facts of such people we eat ourselves sick.

How else to account for the sudden interest in Zweig, this mania, this *craze*—the articles, films, and conferences—but as a kind of madness, of shame? How else to interpret the success of Phelps' book? He cannot sign the copies fast enough. Yet why *Zweig*, why him, why now? What chord has he struck? What tale does his life tell? And how, how it baffles me, is it sufficient, enough? Such a story should never be enough, it should be more than we can bear. Why, just a glimpse of his final days here should make us wretch and stagger, bang our heads, forget to eat, to breathe. It should bring us to our knees.

Even now, as the sales of Phelps' book continue to rise, the presses whirring, the cash registers chiming, even now Zweig's popularity is beginning to flag, our use of him failing, our need of him already on the wane. No doubt Phelps himself can sense it and fears it, he must sign faster and faster, Zweig's life, Zweig's death, soon to be eclipsed by the lives, the tales, of others, perhaps again by Zweig's own, who knows, for a person can always be read *otherwise*.

Surely once we have had our fill of Zweig he will be abandoned, neglected, ignored, he will be forgotten, *forgotten again*, superseded, supplanted, displaced, the unsold copies of Phelps' book swiftly remaindered, dumped at a discount or pulped, when perhaps years later some student in a university library somewhere might happen upon a copy of the book one day, might wonder briefly about Zweig, about his flight and suicide, about his heart-sick, head-sick wife. Book in hand, she might wonder about the rain in the jungle here, about the rain in the jungle at night. She might read the blurbs, skim the flyleaf, she might flip through the photos inside, briefly screwing up her eyes at the grainy old prints, the house from the street, the couple dead in their bed. And if she is moved she might sample a passage here and there to see she what she thinks of the story, the prose. She might sniff the book, she might weigh it like a pot in her hands, only to replace it where she found it. She'll do it quickly, abruptly, for her friend is waiting, she has just received a message, a text; she is late, she lost track of the time, and quickly gathers up her things, her laptop and textbooks, her pencils and notebooks and pens. Already she is distracted by thoughts of her friend (of her, of him), so that already the window on Zweig has closed. Indeed the moment she leaves the building she will not remember the book at all, such is the way these days, even if we followed her out the door to where she is unchaining her bike by the steps and asked her about Zweig, about the book she'd just been looking at, she (she is not defensive: she might smile as she fastens her chinstrap) will only shrug her skinny shoulders and sigh, for she is in hurry, she is sorry, she has plans, she must go.

Even those who have read the book, the agents and editors, the critics and scholars, even Phelps himself, what does he, what do I, what does anyone really know about Zweig, a question to which Freud himself would have said: *Nothing.* In the end we know nothing about him—*maybe less.* For we have tied ourselves up in hypocrisies, concealments, false colorings, and lies; we have tied ourselves in knots. To even the people we know best we remain a mystery in the end, a hull, a husk, the blood of the mystery still circulating, the blood of the mystery still warm. In us they see what they need to see, they snatch what they can, though we cry and shout and stomp our feet, though we wave our arms in the air: *Here I am! Look at me!* And to them we do the same. We need to, we must. We take what we can, we improvise, pay deference, we presume, we make due, for love and envy are nothing if not selfish, blind, our heroes and heretics but the dream-works of our own dull flesh, Plutarch's Pyrrhus not Pyrrhus, Edel's James not

James, Fraser's Mary not Mary, Lee's Woolf not Woolf, Terril's Mao not Mao, Holmes' Shelley not Shelley, Reuth's Goebbels not Goebbels, Wolff's Bach not Bach, Painter's Proust not Proust, even Augustine's *Confessions* but a gracious—a glorious—sham: the child's voice chanting, the pears to the pigs! And that hand, that pale, that beautiful, hand! Saramago knew it well: the slender girl, the soup, the spoon. How to plumb the depths with one shapely, one paralyzed hand?

I begrudge Phelps nothing, I applaud him, I do, though he will never forgive me, I know. He will never understand. Even now the little voice in his head is screeching, it is sounding the alarm, for there is no way he can stop me; there is nothing he can do. Not even if he were on a flight to Rio right now, sipping a whiskey, checking his watch, his phone, not even if his flight were about to land, the cabin lights switched on, the seatbacks returned to their upright positions, his bag and tray table safely stowed, not even if he were the first one off the plane could he make it here on time, could he pass through customs, collect his luggage, and hail a taxi, they are often hard to get, the lines long, the drivers surly, they might refuse to take him, it is late, they might double or triple the fare, so that, by the time he arrived here, by the time the taxi made the long, twisting climb from the sea, I myself would be dead, of Zweig's old house there'd be little left to see.

Of the rum Lurdes brought this morning I now help myself to more, rising stiffly from the table to consider the house across the way, the darkened windows, the boarded doors, the heaps of rubbish in the yard. At last the workmen are gone, their tools stowed, the gate at the foot of the driveway secured.

Come tomorrow they will not remember me. They will not remember the man with the glasses, the man at the fence in his t-shirt and shorts. When pressed by the police, when drawn aside by some reporter from the local television station, they will not recall the features of my face, the shape of my eyes, my nose. They will stammer, they will balk; when asked to describe my behavior, my manner, they will only scratch their sweaty heads. The color of my hair, my skin? They will merely shrug their shoulders and grin.

Only later, days, perhaps weeks later, long after the ruins of the house have been cleared, will an image, some portrait, of me emerge. For in time, and with patience, they—the police, the detectives, the press—will gather up the evidence, the fragments, the bits. Oh how little of a life remains! They will connect and correlate the details, the minutiae, the facts: my books and papers, my wallet, my clothes, the names and photographs on my laptop, my phone, both of which I will leave on my desk here to be found. They will scour my email; like bloodhounds they will track each of my internet searches. And they will interview Lurdes at length, poor Lurdes. She will love it, I know, sitting proudly there in her chair by the window, her little dog in her lap, speaking softly, coyly, allowing her thoughts to wander, expire, to loop back upon them-selves, while chuckling and sighing, while dabbing with a napkin at her lips.

Of all the people who could tell my story, Yaniv, it is she whom I trust. For in time, and in her way, she will tell them everything they need to know about me. She will tell them a story that will make them gasp and wonder, a story that will make them goggle and *think*. For she will withhold nothing, she'll intrigue them, exasperate them, the men in their uniforms, the men in their suits. Everything she can think of to say about me she will say, in whatever order she pleases, only to remark with regret that I never met her son.

This of course they won't write down, they won't bother with such details, checking their watches and nodding their heads, only to press her with discretion, with tact. Gently, doggedly (*no, thank you, no more coffee for me*), they will ask her about my habits, my work, when in time, and with patience, they will ask her about Zweig.

Oh, Zweig, poor shade, good luck to you now!

Where she'll begin with him it is hard to imagine, it is hard to say. She'll likely start with his suits, his shoes, yes, with his favorite alligator shoes… But no, she'll begin with his suicide instead; she won't bother with his clothes or with his novels, his teeth, not even with his wives, his faithful, lonely wives, but will start with his death itself, in this house across the way, what more, what else, what better place to begin than the end? Did they know he was Jewish, she'll ask them, significantly. No, does it matter, they'll say. To which reply she'll shake her head, pressing them hard where they sit there on the couch, there where her husband died, before telling them what little she knows about Zweig and his world, what little (and fantastic) she knows about Jews. And sooner or later she will tell them about you. For in time she will lead them back to Rio, to New York, then to Israel, to Haifa, to you.

I hear a distant rumbling now and check the barometer on the wall, as it often rains heavily in the mountains this time of year, when here in the valley it is clear. Above Zweig's house the sky flickers with light, when a sudden breeze stirs the chimes beside me, riffling the curtains and filling the apartment with the smell of wood smoke and ashes from the clearing up the hill, and with the thick, dark scent of Lurdes' cooking, the coconut milk and soy sauce, the turmeric, *chouriço*, and ghee.

It is one of those perfect evenings one never quite believes, the light, the air, even the people, the trees, all bound together by a web of invisible threads, so that again it seems that anything is possible here, that, should I only wish it now, Yaniv, you yourself would walk in through this door, jostling me with your shoulder, making fun of my sandals, my hair. I would ask for nothing more, but this time it is Lurdes who pushes her way in. She is impatient, I hear Scriabin, when with a banging of her pots and pans the evening proper begins. I get the forks, the glasses, I pull out her chair, though she is far too busy to sit, humming anxiously and flapping her tiny wings.

She looks beautiful tonight, she has changed her dress, her shoes, there is a rusty flush to her cheeks. And she is wearing perfume, a lush, pungent scent, dizzying as ether, heady as gardenias in bloom.

She has just been talking with her son, she tells me, he is having trouble with the priest, an older man with a chip on his shoulder who recently repeated his reservations about their marriage, about the children, the chapel, their faith, though it is none of his damned business, she exclaims to me now, crossing her herself at once. "I mean, *vixe Maria*, is the bloody man a fortuneteller too? Can he see into the future, can he see into their hearts?

"Of course we all know what this is about," she avers with a stern and knowing look. "The girl was married before, so what, who cares, though I'm not to worry, Francisco assures me, it's just the priest's way, he tells me, he swears, the hemming and hawing, the pacing back and forth. He says it's mostly for show, this carrying on. Of all the priests they could find! The old crank. After all, who is he to define God's love?" she cries aloud to me, "the vanity, the nerve, just say the damned prayers, I want to tell him, just do as you're told!" But she has gone too far, she knows, and stumbles to her chair where for a moment she sits there and sighs. Briefly it seems that she will cry, scrunching up her face and twisting the corners of her apron, when abruptly she rises from the table, throwing her arms in the air: "God is everything vexing, God is everything good!"

It is another Étude tonight, one of Scriabin's earliest, a moody, elegiac piece that fills the room around us as we eat, so that the very walls seem to billow and swell.

She knows only little things about him, Vygotsky, that he came from Russia, that he has no family, that he lives on vodka and buttered toast. It has been weeks since she has seen him, his loose, lace-less shoes, his shock of bright white hair. How he does his laundry, how he gets his groceries, she cannot say, she cannot guess.

Now she fears that something in him has changed. He seems sadder, lonelier. She fears that he is dying.

Tonight's is a piece I know well, a piece from my childhood, one I often heard my mother play. Scriabin, under the spell of Chopin, had written it to great acclaim when he was just fifteen years old.

Eager not to miss a note of it tonight, we listen in silence until the piece is over, when Vygotsky begins it again, this time so slowly, so languidly, that it takes me a moment to recognize it. I picture him weeping.

"Was Scriabin a Jew?" Lurdes asks me, after a pause. The question surprises me.

"A Jew? Why do you ask?"

"I don't know. The music, it sounds Jewish to me," she says, arranging the chicken on our plates.

"Well, no, he wasn't Jewish. At least as far as I know. Perhaps it's the Gypsy music you hear. He loved the Gypsy music he used to hear in the streets."

Only then do I remember that his daughter was Jewish, a convert to the faith. "No, Scriabin himself wasn't Jewish, but his daughter Ariadna was. When older she moved to France and married a Jew, a poet and member of the Resistance in World War II. She herself was a hero during the Occupation, though she was still in her teens, having co-founded the fearsome partisan movement known as *Armée Juive*. She was killed near Toulouse in an ambush by the French militia."

At this Lurdes nods her head. "Yes, perhaps that's what I'm hearing," she muses, arranging the chicken on the plates. "Such a brave, tragic girl. She must have suffered so."

"No, no, you couldn't be hearing that, for that all happened later, after Scriabin himself was dead," I protest gently, though she doesn't appear to hear me, to care, pouring herself more rum, which she sips with a pensive smacking of her lips.

"Yes, that must be what I hear."

To pass the time while we eat, and eager to avoid what now seems obvious between us, to even glance at the house across the way for fear she'll confront me at last, for fear she'll try to stop me, dissuade me, I tell her more about Scriabin, about his childhood in Moscow, about the plan I'd had, some years ago, to write a treatment of his life.

"You see, my mother loved Scriabin. I thought I'd write the

book as a gift to her, as a consolation of sorts, though by then she'd given up playing."

'Well, what happened?" says Lurdes. "What happened to the book?"

"I got sick."

"Sick?"

"Yes, the first in a long series of breakdowns. It's a shame, really, for I had just laid the groundwork for the project (I'd outlined the basic chapters and had actually booked a trip to Moscow to visit the archives there), when I got sick," I explain, feeling suddenly, unusually, tired. Again my mouth feels chalky and dry. "In any case, I lacked the musical knowledge to really do justice to his life.

"What had intrigued me initially, perhaps even more than his music itself, was the mysticism behind it. A devoted Theosophist, he—like so many in his day—was passionate about the writings of the occultist and spiritual medium, Helena Blavatsky, who'd spent the better part of her life formulating a broad, esoteric vision of the world that blended the wisdom of the ancient Greeks, of Judaism, Christianity, Freemasonry, and modern science, with that of the great Buddhist and Hindu sages. Scriabin's goal as a composer had proved no less ambitious than hers—and equally preposterous. In his final years he sought nothing less than to interpret the evolution of the universal soul through his music!"

I raise my glass to drink when I set it down again, feeling flushed, dizzy. "Of course in the end he went mad, as all such people do, dying of septicemia in the midst of composing his magnum opus, then but a flurry of cryptic notes—a multi-media work called *Mysterium* that he'd hoped to have performed high in the Himalayas, a grandiose religious synthesis of all of the arts, a musical Armageddon that was to herald the birth of a brave new world. The point is, I never got around to writing the book. It was foolish even to try."

"Nonsense! It's never foolish to try," she scoffs at me, though as if distracted, as if thinking of something else.

Her gestures seem different to me this evening. In the way she moves, in the way she bangs her pots and pans, there is a fitfulness, an agitation, that unnerves me. Twice she has dropped her cooking spoon, twice she has cursed her arthritis, the joints of her fingers like small hard nuts.

I want to calm her, Yaniv, to set her heart at ease. I want to tell her about you, to let her know that you might come looking for her one day, might stop in at the market downstairs to ask about her, that one day, perhaps someday soon, you might climb the stairs at the back of the building here and rap twice on her door. But I don't. Instead I carry the dishes to the table, take her apron from her, then pull out her chair.

Not surprisingly, the food is delicious, or would be, if I didn't feel so nauseous, so sick. I make a show of eating it to please her, but she doesn't want a show, she doesn't care, not at this point, not now, clearing our plates from the table the moment she is done and lighting a cigarette, one of the skinny brown ones she prefers, which she puffs in silence, thinking, listening, when, still looking at the food on her plate, she says, "My father died of cancer, you know. Such a strange, inhuman disease. He twitched a lot, had terrible headaches, sometimes he soiled his pants.

"For some reason he loved to watch us eat, my brother and me," she muses dolefully. "Even in his final days, when he had given up his classes and his students rarely came to see him anymore, to talk with him about poetry and art, even then he tried never to miss a meal with us, though he rarely touched his food, only chuckled at our fighting. We must have fought every night, my brother and me, my brother always trying to get a rise out of him, taunting him at the table with his talk of gambling and liquor and girls, for he too was sick, I see that now. He couldn't bear the idea that his father was dying, he refused it, denied it, once he punched me in the head, threatened to kill me if I mentioned it again. He simply wouldn't have it, staying out late, neglecting his schoolwork, and abusing when not ignoring the man as a guard, a charm, against his death.

"But there are no charms against anything these days—not violence, not loneliness, not sickness or death, and so my brother went on living, he keeps his grief in a drawer somewhere, though I've never found it, I've looked. One day he may never come home, then who knows what I'll do, sell his apartment, his things, São Paulo seems nice, if Francisco would have me, which he would if I asked him, he's a good boy, he would.

"For now we'll just see, one day is up, the next day down, what more can one say for certain than that? And even that, even that is not enough to explain some things, now is it, my father, my husband, your father in the snow, your father in his car on the tracks, just a puzzle really, you try to make the pieces fit, and sometimes a few of the pieces get lost, and sometimes they don't fit at all, like a piece from a different puzzle got mixed in with yours, and now here you are, in Brazil, with all your wondering about your son, wondering right now if he'll ever wonder about you, about who you were, about why you did the things you did. Of course he'll never succeed, he'll never find the answers, you know.

"It's just the way things are, one must love without hope. We do our best, he'll get what he needs, he'll do what he must do. And you, you will climb that hill again tonight. Once I've cleared away these plates, once I've left you alone, you will cross the street here and squeeze your way in through the gate. I've seen the way you do it, the way you scramble your way up that hill. Yes, yes," she murmurs plaintively, as though she can see it right now, my bright white shirt in the darkness on that hill, "once I've cleared the dishes here and left you alone, once I'm back in my apartment and getting ready for bed, brushing my hair, my teeth, maybe watching TV, maybe talking with my son on the phone, you will scramble your way up that hill tonight. You will climb it as you have climbed it before, as you have climbed it every night since you arrived here. You will scramble your way up that hill, stopping just long enough beneath the sagging veranda to catch your breath, to make sure that no has seen you, when, like a moth, you will circle the house until you find your way in.

"And tonight," she tells me, "tonight he'll be expecting you, your Zweig—freshly shaven, perched there like a child on the edge of his bed. Tonight he'll be happy to see you, relieved you've come again, that you've come at last, that the night, *this* night, is finally here, is here again, the packing, the sighing, the longing, the grief. This time he'll be ready for the end, having rehearsed it before the mirror tonight, like a part in a movie, like a part in a play. That is how you'll find him tonight, in his room, on his bed, in his favorite shirtsleeves and tie. He'll have washed his face, combed his hair. And he'll have drawn the blinds, readied the pills and water, he'll have plumped the pillows for his head.

"Then again you might surprise him," she suggests, toying with the chicken on her plate. "You may find he is not expecting you at all. Who knows his state of mind tonight? He could be puzzled by your appearance, your face. Surely he will wonder about the gas can and rags, and about the pistol, my brother's pistol, in the waist of your pants. Why, he might think you've come to kill him, a Nazi agent, that you've been sent by Hitler himself to murder him at last. He may cringe and cower, he may tremble at your step, so that you must be ready to stop him, you mustn't let him panic and choke down the pills, not then, not yet, not with the dog still eating, not with Lotte in the kitchen still in tears on the floor. You must stall him, you must do what you can do, tell him something, anything to distract him, to give you time to find Lotte in the kitchen there, where you must gather her up, the forks and spoons and knives, you must help her to her feet, such women they bloom at the slightest, most negligent touch.

"Tonight," she insists, in a voice that stirs me, a voice I seem to know, "you must suppose that everything you've read about this night is possible, is true. You must suppose, that they have made a pact together, this Lotte and her Zweig, that their love is such that they have chosen to die as one, to die together in that cramped little room, she could never live without him, she knows, but will come from the kitchen when he calls her, she will swallow her pills, *good girl, brave girl,* he will smile, kiss her cheek, pat her lightly on the knee.

"Picture them there tonight: she is wearing the kimono he likes, he likes the feel of it, so cool, so smooth, like water, like silk. He asks her: *Did you return the cookbook to Feders' wife?* A question that makes Lotte scowl, makes her scoff: *How she fusses, that shrew!*—a slight (so unexpected from her) that finally snaps the tension between them, makes them snigger, makes them laugh so hard they weep!

"Why they could say anything now, now that she has opened the box, now that she has pulled her thumb from the dike. They could howl and scream and stomp their feet, they could smash the dishes and pictures, why not? They could tear night sky with their cries, but already they draw themselves back, they draw themselves in, embarrassed, abashed, when he looks at her askance, strokes his moustache, his chin.

"For she cannot look at him now, no," says Lurdes now, "but studies the floor instead, as if she might sniffle, might cry, he is iron, she is ribbon and thread, the air so still tonight she can smell his sweat, his moldy shirt, his oily, unwashed hair, the smell of dying, she thinks, a kind of oozing, it seems, so that she sniffs her fingers, her dress: the dog, a little dish soap, is all. She wonders vaguely: perhaps a woman's death is different, no scent, no fragrance at all, but the thought doesn't catch, she hasn't the will to pursue it just now and locks the door behind them, the night hot, the bed narrow, wondering what it is he smells right now, if he smells anything at all, her cheek on his chest, her hand on his neatly clasped hands. She thinks she can smell the rain, pictures it sweeping down from the mountains, she can almost feel the coolness on her skin and allows her eyes to wander about the drably papered walls of their room as if she might find the coolness there, in the corner, on the shelf, maybe curled like a cat on the chair. She is tired, more tired than she thought, she knew, the heat, the errands this morning, the fruitless running around, that woman who was shouting at the clerk in town. Strange morning—every woman with a baby at her breast!

"Who knows what she'll think about? The rain, the neighbors. Maybe she herself was a miserable baby," says Lurdes, as if testing the water in bath. "Maybe she cried a lot, the colic, the rashes. Maybe her teeth came in too fast, so that now she feels them with a finger where she lies there beside him, thinks briefly of brushing them, but hasn't the strength, the will, she can hardly feel her legs at all, suddenly so drowsy, so weak, that even her arm on his chest—how even to turn her wrist to see the time," murmurs Lurdes now, eyelids fluttering, a look of rapture on her small, wan face, "when gently—there's the rain now—she closes her eyes to sleep…"

She is quiet for a moment, and it seems she is about to get up and go, that she is done with me at last, when she snorts, roughly stubbing out her cigarette. "Yes, you might very well suppose that, that that was the way it happened. Or you might suppose something else," she presses me firmly, coldly, "something altogether different, a story much harder to reckon, to bear, say, that Lotte is there in the bedroom with him tonight, this night, that night *then*, that she is there with him now, to comfort him and console him, the wretched, helpless man, not weeping in the kitchen after all, but there at his side, stroking his hand, his head, humming a simple tune to him, perhaps reading aloud to him a favorite passage from one of their many long letters from home. Who knows how you'll find her there tonight? She might be reading or sleeping, she might be pulling out her hair, why, for all you know she might still be in Rio with their friends, why not, surely she deserves to get away, to live her life, the forks and spoons and knives! What has she to return to here, the anguish, the fretting, why, she might have wished him dead. Did you ever think of that? She could have stayed in England, you know, she was really quite pretty. She might have married a banker, a lawyer, spent her days wandering the streets of London in a pretty new dress. She might have had kids by now, some little girl to dote on, a peaceful little house and garden. She might have been a singer, a teacher, a nurse, no one ever thinks of that, do they, the things that could have been? I mean the girl was nearly thirty years his junior! She hardly stood a chance, poor thing, closed her eyes for a kiss and woke up here, in that house, with *him*, that frog, that *prince*, typing his notes, rinsing his underwear, and polishing his fancy shoes. She must have hated the daily rounds of chess, the sulking and scolding, his endless groaning about his writing, his teeth. She must have hated the bats and mosquitos, the monkeys screeching all day in the trees, she must have loathed her little life here, for she hadn't a penny of her own, you know, the people frightened her, the rain, so that she rarely left the house but to cross the road to the little market down the way, where she often stood aghast before the mounds of ripe fruit, where she sometimes burst into tears.

"She'd liked the little library here," says Lurdes now, parting the curtain to consider the women below. "My mother told me that she sometimes saw her there, just sitting by herself, where she'd gone to return her husband's books, not reading, only thinking where she sat at one of the wooden carrels between the bookshelves, sighing, twisting her rings, some history or novel opened flat on the desk before her, though she rarely read anything, not there, only gazed out through the windows at the dark, suffocating trees, breathing calmly, gently, for the dust there didn't bother her, as it did in the house, as it had in in their villa in Bath. She'd liked the fusty old smell of the books and of the varnish on the desks and chairs.

She'd liked the hush and coolness of the place, the lazy old fans, the charts and maps and globes, the fact that no one, not even the librarian, expected her to speak. She must have felt she could live a whole bright life just sitting there alone, gazing at the ranks of dully colored spines and staring blindly at the trees.

"She was smart, she knew she was smart, as a child she'd been recklessly praised. She'd been bound to disappoint, so that there were days when it nearly made sense to her (she thought she saw a kind of logic in it) that she should be sitting there alone in that dusty little library some thousands of miles from home. Such things it pleased her to think about, to know, like a deal she had made with herself, a truce of which she spoke to no one, never even whispered it aloud, only admired it like a bauble, a jewel, as she drowsed before some fiction there, sometimes thinking about her mother's Bakelite brooch, sometimes stroking the lock, a keepsake, of her niece's fine hair.

"For all her weeping, for all her self-pity, there was little that surprised her anymore. She didn't have to like it, it was enough just to know, to be able take one's bearings and sigh. In which case she would never have wished him dead, it's true," remarks Lurdes now, as if as a concession to me, to something certain I'd said. "It would never have occurred to her to blame *him* for her life there. She was young and frightened, she'd been properly raised, so that maybe you're right to think that she would never have confronted him, the celebrity, the man, never have wished to, have dared, openly delighting in his jokes, his interests, admiring his suits and shoes, and cherishing his books (his books!), which she could never quite manage to read, to press her way through, *to believe*, the paralyzed girl in the castle, the wretched young post office clerk. Every time she took up one of his novels to read it she tightened up inside, like a screw, so that it was harder than ever to breathe. Trapped here in this jungle, this town, she must have hated his precious stories, some of which she'd typed for him, some of which he'd read aloud to their friends, when they'd gathered on the veranda at night, she must have cringed at what had seemed to her, always, each time she'd heard them, each time she'd tried to read them herself, his shameless, nearly desperate desire *to please*. And always his voice—that same starchy voice—in her head.

"Yet she would never have blamed him, no," remarks Lurdes. "She would have blamed herself instead, her laziness and ignorance, her cooking, her asthma, her moods, for who was she to throw stones, she was no one, a woman, she was far too silly for that.

"Even when he talked, when he spoke to her at night, even when his lips moved, when he was looking right at her, she must have felt a ghost afloat in her chair, for he often talked straight through her, beyond her, he must have, he did, he must have talked right past her, at night, to the puddles of air that collected round her head. With all her might she would have bitten her tongue when he prattled on about the world, *his* world, *that* world, as they sat together on the wide covered terrace, as he paced behind her while she knitted or typed, the ties cut, the voyage made, there was no turning back, so that perhaps she'd learned to love him after all, his voice, his self-pity, the cloying stench of his sweat, perhaps for her his grief was enough, that she had found a way to grow full *within* it, as some wives do, nursing it with patience until it flowered, a happy ending, their deaths, a burst bud, a bright if noxious bloom...

"But no, no!" she cries now, hammering the table with her fists.

Her face is strained, I see the tendons in her neck. "Not even you could believe that," she assails me with a force, a vehemence, that startles me. "Not even you could tell me that she was happy here, poor girl, that she'd gladly wasted her youth for him, for such a bitter, broken man, that when finally he'd told her the time had come she'd offered not a word of protest, so blind was her love for him, so certain her faith, sitting obediently as a child beside him and swallowing her measure of pills. Why she must have loathed the man! Yet what choice did she have? Even if he wasn't a Nazi he never loved her, he never really cared for her at all, it's true! He never even mentioned her in the note he left behind him, did he, no *we*, no *us*, he used her, don't you see? He never had any intention of taking her with him, happy to leave her here where he had brought her, trapped her, here in this house, this jungle, so helplessly far from home. He swallowed the pills without telling her a thing, every last one of them, before lying down for his usual nap. Wake me in an hour, I'll peel the potatoes, he told her, he *must* have told her, he must have said something like that, anything at all to distract her, to confuse her suspicions, her fears, casually plumping his pillows before removing his shoes, so that what choice did she have when she found him dead but to kill herself, too, *but how, with what,* yanking open the cupboards and pulling out the drawers, the detergents, the knives, finally swallowing what remained of the poison they kept by the sink, it was all she could find, some nasty old poison for ants, choking it down, gagging, spitting, stumbling blindly to the bed where he lay, so that by the time the maid arrived the next morning and found the door locked, by the time the gardener fetched his ladder, climbed onto the roof, loosened the tiles, and looked in, by the time the police arrived with their cameras and kits, it must have seemed a death for the movies, the stage...

"Still I hope that I'm wrong, I do," she whispers now, face slack and pale. She seems smaller somehow, as if suddenly drained of her conviction, her strength. "I hope that when you scramble your way up that hill tonight you will find them together there, whispering, holding hands, maybe weeping softly where they sit on the edge of the bed, listening to the voice of the night as it closes in around them, the tram, the monkeys, the rain clouds, the wind. I'd prefer such an ending to mine."

I am about to speak when she stops me with her hand. "Yes, I'd prefer that, I would but you'll find what you'll find, the truth is always true, so that should you discover him there in his bedroom alone, as I suspect, as I am certain you will, you must leave him where he is, no drama, no pity, he will do what he must do. And you, you must look to Lotte instead," she commands me, squeezing my hand. "You must seek her in the kitchen where you will find her after all, she is young (the crash, the silverware). Such women, the weeping, they always mean well.

"Before you burn that house down you must crouch there beside her on the kitchen floor, you must help her to gather up the silverware, the forks and spoons and knives. Then you must take her by the elbow, the hand, she will not be frightened, she will not resist you, be gentle, be firm. Take her lightly by the elbow and guide her out onto the veranda from where you must show her the planets, the stars—there Venus, there Perseus, there Gemini and Taurus, for even with the light of the flames you will find them in the sky tonight. Show her Sirius, Canis Major. Just look for the brightest star, then follow the hunter's belt. She will cling to you,

you must hold her and grieve, for there is nothing you can tell her now, there is nothing you can do."

With that Lurdes looks hard at me, as if searching my eyes for a sign, only to scowl and turn away. I try to think of something lasting to say but can only watch her as she scrapes the plates then stacks them with a clatter on the tray by the door.

Alone again I make one last tour of the rooms, as one does before leaving a hotel room or a cottage by the sea. I raise the blinds, I open the windows, I check for socks beneath the bed.

I am happy, Yaniv, I am, and for the first time I am scared, for one can never imagine the end. By necessity it deceives one, a cloak, a veil, a conjurer's trick, for surely tomorrow will come, it has always come, it must, so that what else can I suppose but that, come daylight, come dawn, I will scramble my way down that hill again and slip back into my apartment here, where I will strip off my shorts, get a drink of water, then climb into bed.

Even as I know better I simply have to believe that tomorrow I will be roused, as I have been roused each morning, by the raucous clatter of the grilles on the shop front below, and by the usual crowd of lonely, unsprung women, who will gather here on the sidewalk with their broken-backed sandals and poorly dyed hair, with their bloated arms and breasts, talking of husbands and dish soap and squinting up at the parched, still implacable sky. And as ever I will revel in their voices, the crickets and spiders, the rushing of water, the creaking of windows and doors.

As surely as the sun has set tonight I will see it rise again tomorrow. I will wake to the reckless, happy chatter of children bound for school, hear the sputter of trucks and motorbikes as they climb the long hill past my building, hear the bus at the corner with its long hydraulic hiss. Dogs will bark, the pipes will gurgle, when like a sign from the gods there will come the familiar sounds from next door, the humming and cursing, the banging of pots and pans, and soon Lurdes will be knocking at my door, she will pour us some coffee, we will sit by the window and talk—of the landlord and his mistresses, of the chances of rain, of the price in the paper of mangoes and beef. She'll be near to bursting tomorrow, she'll have so much to tell me, she'll have so much to say.

Death won't touch me, I think, but will join us at the table here, where he will laugh a little (goodnight, sweet boy), where he will swallow a mouthful of rum.

Acknowledgements

I am pleased to acknowledge Kristina Michahelles at Casa Zweig for the permission to reproduce the cover photograph of Stefan and Lotte Zweig's house in Petrópolis, Brazil, as well as the photographs of the Zweigs within the house itself. I am grateful for her support. For the photograph of the front hallway of my old house (18) I thank my aunt, Lisa Mescon. I thank Pushkin Press for permission to reprint Allan Blunden's translation of Stefan Zweig's poem "Der Sechzigjährige dankt" (25) from their book *Three Lives: A Biography of Stefan Zweig* by Oliver Matuschek, and for the use of the lengthy passage from Stefan Zweig's biography, *Marie Antoinette* (28). Both books proved instrumental to my work. Additionally, I would like to recognize the Brazilian Institute of Geography and Statistics for the list of Brazilian skin tones and colors (27), which I discovered in the marvelous book, *The Brazil Reader: History, Culture, Politics*, edited by Robert M. Levine and John J. Crocitti and published by Duke University Press. For the photograph of the boy on the pony (50)I thank "born1945". I am grateful to W. W. Norton & Company for granting me permission to reprint a segment of the poem "From the Painting Back from Market by Chardin" (53), copyright © 1967 by Eavan Boland, from *New Collected Poems* by Eavan Boland. I am thankful to the people at Ariadne Press for permitting me to reprint the short excerpts from Zweig's book, *Brazil: A Land of the Future* (62), translated by Lowell A. Bangerter. Also, I would like to express my gratitude to the people at Bloomsbury/Continuum Press for allowing me to reprint the excerpt from one of Zweig's letters from their remarkable book, *Stefan and Lotte Zweig's South American Letters: New York, Argentina and Brazil, 1940-42* (63), edited by Darién J. Davis and Oliver Marshall. Lastly, I would like to express my gratitude to the people at Oxford University Press for allowing me to use a passage from Machado de Assis' extraordinary novel *The Posthumous Memoirs of Brás Cubas* (89).

For my understanding of Stefan Zweig himself, I would like to acknowledge my debt to his many fine biographers, including Donald A. Prater, Elizabeth Allday, Friderike Zweig, Oliver Matuschek, Volker Weidermann, and George Prochnik, as well as to poet, critic, essayist, and translator Michael Hofmann for his bold and insightful dissent. Additionally, for helping me fine-tune my sense of biography as a practice, as a whole, I am grateful to Richard Holmes for his illuminating book, *This Long Pursuit*, to Paula Backscheider for her *Reflections on Biography*, to Nigel Hamilton for his *Biography: A Brief History*, and to Scott Donaldson, whose thoughtful study, *The Impossible Craft: Literary Biography*, proved a boon to me in the completion of my own.

For their support and encouragement I thank Marc Estrin and Donna Bister at Fomite Press, to whom I am more grateful than I can express. For their help with the Portuguese and German in this novel, I'd like to thank my friends, Alex Sousa and Sibylle Schlesier, respectively. Moreover I wish to thank my sons, Ezra and Isaiah, my mother, Linda Rennie Forcey, my sister, Maggie Nash, and my brother, Charles Forcey for their love, support, and inspiration. Finally, I am indebted to my friends and readers, George Ovitt, Cynde Moore, David Gutierrez—and of course, as ever, to my brilliant and incomparable wife, Dr. Annie Kirkpatrick Nash.

About Fomite

A fomite is a medium capable of transmitting infectious organisms from one individual to another.

"The activity of art is based on the capacity of people to be infected by the feelings of others." Tolstoy, *What Is Art?*

Writing a review on Amazon, Good Reads, Shelfari, Library Thing or other social media sites for readers will help the progress of independent publishing. To submit a review, go to the book page on any of the sites and follow the links for reviews. Books from independent presses rely on reader to reader communications.

For more information or to order any of our books, visit
http://www.fomitepress.com/FOMITE/Our_Books.html

More Titles from Fomite...

Novels

Joshua Amses — *During This, Our Nadir*
Joshua Amses — *Raven or Crow*
Joshua Amses — *The Moment Before an Injury*
Jaysinh Birjepatel — *The Good Muslim of Jackson Heights*
Jaysinh Birjepatel — *Nothing Beside Remains*
David Brizer — *Victor Rand*
Paula Closson Buck — *Summer on the Cold War Planet*
Dan Chodorkoff — *Loisaida*
David Adams Cleveland — *Time's Betrayal*
Jaimee Wriston Colbert — *Vanishing Acts*
Roger Coleman — *Skywreck Afternoons*
Marc Estrin — *Hyde*
Marc Estrin — *Kafka's Roach*

Fomite

Marc Estrin — *Speckled Vanities*
Zdravka Evtimova — *In the Town of Joy and Peace*
Zdravka Evtimova — *Sinfonia Bulgarica*
Daniel Forbes — *Derail This Train Wreck*
Greg Guma — *Dons of Time*
Richard Hawley — *The Three Lives of Jonathan Force*
Lamar Herrin — *Father Figure*
Michael Horner — *Damage Control*
Ron Jacobs — *All the Sinners Saints*
Ron Jacobs — *Short Order Frame Up*
Ron Jacobs — *The Co-conspirator's Tale*
Scott Archer Jones — *A Rising Tide of People Swept Away*
Julie Justicz — *A Boy Called Home*
Maggie Kast — *A Free Unsullied Land*
Darrell Kastin — *Shadowboxing with Bukowski*
Coleen Kearon — *Feminist on Fire*
Coleen Kearon — *#triggerwarning*
Jan Englis Leary — *Thicker Than Blood*
Diane Lefer — *Confessions of a Carnivore*
Rob Lenihan — *Born Speaking Lies*
Colin Mitchell — *Roadman*
Ilan Mochari — *Zinsky the Obscure*
Peter Nash — *Parsimony*
Peter Nash — *The Perfection of Things*
Gregory Papadoyiannis — *The Baby Jazz*
Andy Potok — *My Father's Keeper*
Kathryn Roberts — *Companion Plants*
Robert Rosenberg — *Isles of the Blind*
Fred Russell — *Rafi's World*
Ron Savage — *Voyeur in Tangier*
David Schein — *The Adoption*
Lynn Sloan — *Principles of Navigation*
L.E. Smith — *The Consequence of Gesture*

Fomite

L.E. Smith — *Travers' Inferno*
L.E. Smith — *Untimely RIPped*
Bob Sommer — *A Great Fullness*
Tom Walker — *A Day in the Life*
Susan V. Weiss —*My God, What Have We Done?*
Peter M. Wheelwright — *As It Is On Earth*
Suzie Wizowaty — *The Return of Jason Green*

Poetry

Anna Blackmer — *Hexagrams*
Antonello Borra — *Alfabestiario*
Antonello Borra — *AlphaBetaBestiaro*
Sue Burton — *Little Steel*
David Cavanagh— *Cycling in Plato's Cave*
James Connolly — *Picking Up the Bodies*
Greg Delanty — *Loosestrife*
Mason Drukman — *Drawing on Life*
J. C. Ellefson — *Foreign Tales of Exemplum and Woe*
Tina Escaja — *Caida Libre/Free Fall*
Anna Faktorovich — *Improvisational Arguments*
Barry Goldensohn — *Snake in the Spine, Wolf in the Heart*
Barry Goldensohn — *The Hundred Yard Dash Man*
Barry Goldensohn — *The Listener Aspires to the Condition of Music*
R. L. Green — When — *You Remember Deir Yassin*
Kate Magill — *Roadworthy Creature, Roadworthy Craft*
Tony Magistrale — *Entanglements*
Andreas Nolte — *Mascha: The Poems of Mascha Kaléko*
Sherry Olson — *Four-Way Stop*
David Polk — *Drinking the River*
Phliip Ramp — *The Melancholy Of A Life As The Joy Of Living It Slowly Chills*
Janice Miller Potter — *Meanwell*
Joseph D. Reich — *Connecting the Dots to Shangrila*

Fomite

Joseph D. Reich — *The Hole That Runs Through Utopia*
Joseph D. Reich — *The Housing Market*
Joseph D. Reich — *The Derivation of Cowboys and Indians*
Kennet Rosen and Richard Wilson — *Gomorrah*
Fred Rosenblum — *Vietnumb*
David Schein — *My Murder and Other Local News*
Harold Schweizer — *Miriam's Book*
Scott T. Starbuck — *Industrial Oz*
Scott T. Starbuck — *Hawk on Wire*
Seth Steinzor — *Among the Lost*
Seth Steinzor — *To Join the Lost*
Susan Thomas — *The Empty Notebook Interrogates Itself*
Susan Thomas — *In the Sadness Museum*
Paolo Valesio and Todd Portnowitz — *Midnight in Spoleto*
Sharon Webster — *Everyone Lives Here*
Tony Whedon — *The Tres Riches Heures*
Tony Whedon — *The Falkland Quartet*
Claire Zoghb — *Dispatches from Everest*

Stories

Jay Boyer — *Flight*
Michael Cocchiarale — *Still Time*
Michael Cocchiarale — *Here Is Ware*
Neil Connelly — *In the Wake of Our Vows*
Catherine Zobal Dent — *Unfinished Stories of Girls*
Zdravka Evtimova — *Carts and Other Stories*
John Michael Flynn — *Off to the Next Wherever*
Derek Furr — *Semitones*
Derek Furr — *Suite for Three Voices*
Elizabeth Genovise — *Where There Are Two or More*
Andrei Guriuanu — *Body of Work*
Zeke Jarvis — *In A Family Way*

Fomite

Jan Englis Leary — *Skating on the Vertical*
Marjorie Maddox — *What She Was Saying*
William Marquess — *Boom-shacka-lacka*
Gary Miller — *Museum of the Americas*
Jennifer Anne Moses — *Visiting Hours*
Martin Ott — *Interrogations*
Jack Pulaski — *Love's Labours*
Charles Rafferty — *Saturday Night at Magellan's*
Ron Savage — *What We Do For Love*
Fred Skolnik— *Americans and Other Stories*
Lynn Sloan — *This Far Isn't Far Enough*
L.E. Smith — *Views Cost Extra*
Caitlin Hamilton Summie — *To Lay To Rest Our Ghosts*
Susan Thomas — *Among Angelic Orders*
Tom Walker — *Signed Confessions*
Silas Dent Zobal — *The Inconvenience of the Wings*

Odd Birds

Micheal Breiner — *the way none of this happened*
J. C. Ellefson — *Under the Influence*
David Ross Gunn — *Cautionary Chronicles*
Andrei Guriuanu — *The Darkest City*
Gail Holst-Warhaft — *The Fall of Athens*
Roger Leboitz — *A Guide to the Western Slopes and the Outlying Area*
dug Nap— *Artsy Fartsy*
Delia Bell Robinson — *A Shirtwaist Story*
Peter Schumann — *Bread & Sentences*
Peter Schumann — *Charlotte Salomon*
Peter Schumann — *Faust 3*
Peter Schumann — *Planet Kasper, Volumes One and Two*
Peter Schumann — *We*

Fomite

Plays
Stephen Goldberg — *Screwed and Other Plays*
Michele Markarian — *Unborn Children of America*

Essays
Robert Sommer — *Losing Francis*